W9-AVB-046

"Call the police!"

"Yes, call the police!" Rory agreed. "But I'll take half an hour's head start. If I can't get the story spread across the newspapers, my name's not Rory Grayson."

Joanna had sudden visions of sensational tabloid stories. "Don't call the police!" she yelled.

"You heard the lady. Don't call the police," Rory reiterated strongly. "Will someone please open the door for me and summon the elevator?"

He strode into the reception area, still carrying Joanna firmly in his arms.

"Your appointments, Mr. Grayson! What will I do? What will I say?" cried the young woman behind the reception desk.

"Say I'm off for the dirtiest weekend that any man could hope to have. That will satisfy everybody."

He strode into the waiting elevator and grinned with wicked satisfaction as the doors slid shut.

EMMA DARCY nearly became an actress until her fiancé declared he preferred to attend the theater *with* her. She became a wife and mother. Later, she took up oil painting—unsuccessfully, she remarks. Then she tried architecture, designing the family home in New South Wales. Next came romance writing—"the hardest and most challenging of all the activities," she confesses.

Don't miss any of our special offers. Write to us at the following address for information on our newest releases.

Harlequin Reader Service
P.O. Box 1397, Buffalo, NY 14240
Canadian address: P.O. Box 603,
Fort Erie, Ont. L2A 5X3

EMMA DARCY

A Wedding To Remember

Harlequin Books

TORONTO • NEW YORK • LONDON
AMSTERDAM • PARIS • SYDNEY • HAMBURG
STOCKHOLM • ATHENS • TOKYO • MILAN
MADRID • WARSAW • BUDAPEST • AUCKLAND

If you purchased this book without a cover you should be aware that this book is stolen property. It was reported as "unsold and destroyed" to the publisher, and neither the author nor the publisher has received any payment for this "stripped book."

ISBN 0-373-11659-4

A WEDDING TO REMEMBER

Copyright © 1993 by Emma Darcy.

All rights reserved. Except for use in any review, the reproduction or utilization of this work in whole or in part in any form by any electronic, mechanical or other means, now known or hereafter invented, including xerography, photocopying and recording, or in any information storage or retrieval system, is forbidden without the written permission of the publisher, Harlequin Enterprises Limited, 225 Duncan Mill Road, Don Mills, Ontario, Canada M3B 3K9.

All characters in this book have no existence outside the imagination of the author and have no relation whatsoever to anyone bearing the same name or names. They are not even distantly inspired by any individual known or unknown to the author, and all incidents are pure invention.

This edition published by arrangement with Harlequin Enterprises B. V.

® and ™ are trademarks of the publisher. Trademarks indicated with ® are registered in the United States Patent and Trademark Office, the Canadian Trade Marks Office and other countries.

Printed in U.S.A.

CHAPTER ONE

AS SHE MADE her first morning cup of coffee, Joanna Harding totted the days up in her mind. Four gone, nine to go. Today was Friday. A week tomorrow was the deadline. Before Brad flew back to Sydney from his conference in Brisbane, she had to decide whether to marry him or not.

Joanna sat down at the table in her mother's kitchen and hunched over her coffee mug, berating herself for not being clear-minded about the future Brad was offering her. There should be no question about what she wanted. Brad was everything Rory Grayson wasn't, yet her failed marriage to Rory cast long, haunting shadows that still affected her.

It was *not her fault* the marriage had failed. The blame lay fairly and squarely on Rory's head. And another part of his anatomy. It was absurd and self-defeating to let his failure cloud her future.

Three years had passed since she had separated from Rory. She had told her ex-husband on the day of their divorce, two years ago, and she had told herself repeatedly since then, that she would never see him again. She did not *want* Rory Grayson to take up another second of her life.

Wanting, however, was one thing, reality quite another. It was as though Rory sat on her shoulder, a white angel who dimmed the attraction of any other man she met, or a dark angel who reminded her of the black pits an intimate relationship could lead her into. It did not seem to matter that her love for him had been crushed under the unforgivable weight of what had happened.

The dust of it still clung around her heart, taunting her with the loss of its substance.

"Do you have any plans for today, Joanna?" her mother asked as she carried her habitual boiled egg and toast breakfast to the table.

Today was the day to blow the dust of Rory Grayson away, Joanna decided. She needed to rid herself of it. Rory had to be buried in a final resting place. If she saw him again and felt nothing, if he left her completely cold, then she could go ahead and accept Brad's proposal, and marry him with a free heart. No hangovers from the past. No regrets. Nothing to spoil her happiness.

"I might give Poppy Dalton a call," she answered her mother. "See if she wants to take in a movie or look around the shops in the city."

It was a safe reply, and she might well spend part of the day with her friend and fellow teacher. It also avoided any mention of Rory. There was nothing to be gained in sparking off an unpleasant and totally unnecessary scene with her mother.

As far as Fay Harding was concerned, the worst thing Joanna had ever done was to marry Rory Grayson, and the best thing she had ever done was divorce him, vindicating Fay's deep and abiding disapproval of him. Right from the start Rory had earned that disapproval by flouting or mocking the rules Fay held dear. Which, of course, had been one of his strong attractions to Joanna, who had bridled against those very same rules all her young life.

Was it rebellion that had drawn her to link her life with Rory's? A heady sense of freedom from all the constrictions of convention? She had believed she had found her true soul mate in Rory, but it hadn't turned out that way.

To Joanna's mind, no matter what the stresses and strains in a marriage, nothing, absolutely nothing, excused adultery. Particularly when that adultery was proven, beyond any possible belief in Rory's denials, by the other woman's pregnancy. It made no difference that the pregnancy was eventually terminated by a miscarriage. The betrayal went too deep for Joanna to ever accept Rory back as her husband.

"You must be missing Brad," her mother remarked, a fondly hopeful note in her voice. As a marriage prospect for her daughter, Brad Latham had Fay Harding's gold-star approval. "It's such a pity he has to be away for the whole midyear break."

"It's a very important conference, Mum," Joanna replied with a resigned shrug, defending his decision while ignoring the probe into her private feelings about Brad.

"I thought he might have asked you to go with him," her mother commented wistfully.

"Not appropriate."

Unlike Rory, who wouldn't have given a damn, Brad would never think of behaving in any way that might draw the censure of others. A discreet affair was one thing, advertising it quite another. Brad's whole life had been governed by a rule book. Ten years in the navy had set a pattern of discipline he had taken straight into the education system. He was totally dependable. And predictable. Important assets in giving her a sense of security, Joanna assured herself.

"Well, you are on his staff," her mother said, piqued into justifying her personal wishes by the abrupt tone of her daughter's reply.

"The conference is for the principals of private schools, Mum. Not the teachers. Brad will be busy politicking the whole time. You know they want to press the government for bigger subsidies next year."

"Yes, but surely they have some time off for socialising," her mother argued.

"It wouldn't look good for Brad to have me there," Joanna explained. "I'm not his wife. And Brad is far too ambitious to put a foot out of line."

Brad had his eye on the headmastership of a more prestigious private school on the other side of Sydney. Relatively young, at thirty-eight, full of drive and energy, a charismatic leader to both pupils and parents, he had a better than even chance of winning the position when it fell vacant at the end of next year.

"There's nothing wrong with ambition, Joanna."

The terse note in her mother's voice drew her gaze. Their eyes clashed for one unguarded moment, and Joanna knew her mother was thinking of Rory and his grievous lack of what Fay Harding recognised as proper ambition. It was her dogmatic opinion that trying out new ideas had no solid substance and could only be regarded as suspicious business.

Joanna neutralised the dangerous ground with a bland reply. "I didn't say there *was* anything wrong with ambition, Mum."

End of argument, if it could be called an argument. For the sake of peace between them, Rory's name was never spoken. Joanna had made that rule when she had come back home.

Her widowed mother had needed help at the time. Her recovery after an operation on a faulty heart valve was slow, and her more favoured daughter, Jessica, had had her hands full with a new baby. Since Joanna had parted from Rory, it was easier for her to step in, easy to stay, even after her mother had regained her full strength and was perfectly capable of coping alone.

Moving to a place of her own would have required thought and effort, and Joanna couldn't summon the interest to bother. Nothing seemed to matter after her break-up with Rory. Apart from which, her mother's home in Burwood was convenient to the school in Strathfield where Joanna taught.

It was easier to live from day to day in a relatively undemanding routine, easy to sink into an emotional limbo where not even her mother's narrow attitudes irritated her. On a superficial level they were company for each other. Besides, after the seven-year rift caused by her marriage to Rory, the reconciliation with her mother was comforting, taking the edge off her loneliness.

It was Brad who had lifted her out of the passivity she had fallen into, giving her a more active interest in life. A positive focus. He was good for her. Good *to* her, as well. They shared the day-to-day happenings at the school, played tennis at weekends, went to concerts and plays together.

He might not be a madly exciting lover, but Brad *was* offering her the problem-free security she had never had in her first marriage. This looking back to what she had once shared with Rory was stupid, yet she had been doing it continually ever since Brad had left for the conference.

It had to stop.

Her mother rose from the table and took her breakfast things to the sink.

"I'll do the washing up after I've eaten, Mum," Joanna quickly offered. "It'll give you a few more minutes with Jessica before she leaves for tennis," she added with a persuasive smile.

Her mother returned a fond look, not really for Joanna. It was more in thought of her other daughter, who was the light of her life. Jessica had done everything right, especially marrying a dentist who was a *professional* man. He was also a pillar of rectitude in providing a good home for his wife and being a splendid husband and father.

"I really enjoy my day with the children," her mother said.

And why not? Joanna thought with dry irony. She had two beautiful granddaughters to spoil while Jessica played tennis, and the little girls were already moulded into the kind of little girls their grandmother approved of. Joanna idly wondered how well her mother would handle a rambunctious little boy.

"Give them my love," she said, encouraging her mother to be on her way.

She was already dressed to go in a smart forest-green pant-suit. Her pearl brooch was precisely positioned at the throat of her beige blouse, pearl earrings in her lobes. There was not a hair out of place in the short white waves that framed her face. Apart from lipstick, which she would undoubtedly apply at the hall mirror near the front door, her make-up was perfectly in place. Fay Harding judged others on appearance, and never would she drop her own standards, not even to mind children.

How she had hated Rory in his scruffy university clothes! And the unshaven stubble that he hadn't bothered about before calling by to see Joanna!

"Have a nice day, dear."

"I will, Mum," Joanna replied with no inner conviction whatsoever.

As she waited to hear the front door closing behind her mother, Joanna considered various plans of action. The telephone directory would give her the information she needed, but if she called Rory, he would undoubtedly take savage satisfaction in reminding her of her last words to him, that they had nothing more to say to each other.

He would hang up on her with the same relentless decisiveness she had displayed in showing him to the door out of her life after their last bitter showdown before the divorce went through.

Besides, she did not want to talk to him. Seeing him would serve her purpose, and the more impersonally she could achieve that, the better. The best place would definitely be in his office. Surely she could work out some way to finagle a few private minutes with him. She mentally practised some lines to justify such a visit.

No grudges, Rory. I'm getting married again. I hope you'll find someone you can be happy with, too.

The decisive door click of her mother's departure spurred Joanna into action. She looked up the market research listings in the telephone directory and had no difficulty in finding the company she was looking for. She circled the number, noted down the new business address in Chatswood and paused to wonder if that was an up-market or down-market move from Rory's last premises in North Sydney. Had his business grown or slumped since the divorce?

With an impatient shake of the head, Joanna dismissed this irrelevant speculation. She was *not* interested in what had happened to Rory. Or why. She simply wanted to see him one more time. That was all. The question she needed answered was whether or not he was at his office today.

Having thought her way around the problem for several minutes, Joanna dialled the number, intent on playing whatever response she got by ear.

"Grayson and Associates," a woman's voice piped cheerfully. "How can I help you?"

"Is Mr. Grayson in today?" Joanna asked.

"Who's calling, please?"

That put Joanna on the spot. Giving her name would almost certainly defeat her purpose. A wild invention leapt into her mind.

"I'm calling for Mr. Kawowski of Matchmakers Incorporated," she rattled out, wondering if it was some kind of Freudian slip to think of a fabricated dating service as a means to get to Rory. "He wants to know if Mr. Grayson would be free to see him later this morning."

"Mr. Grayson is in a meeting right now. Can I ring back to confirm?"

"Would you hold on a moment?" Joanna counted to ten then said, "Sorry. Mr. Kawowski has decided to use another company. Thank you for your time."

She put down the receiver and heaved a sigh of relief. Mission accomplished. No more shillyshallying over the past or the future. Her course of action was decided. Rory Grayson was about to receive an unexpected visitor.

CHAPTER TWO

THE ULTRA-MODERN office building in Chatswood was impressive, but Joanna was not certain it was an up-market move for Rory until she arrived on the floor occupied by his company. When they parted three years ago, he was managing everything himself with a casual staff of five. One glance at the layout of his present premises told her that his business had greatly expanded.

From the reception room, a glass-panelled wall revealed a veritable hive of industry. A huge open area was broken into partitioned computer cubicles with people busy in all of those she could see. At the far end was a row of more private offices for executive staff.

Joanna could not help marvelling over the evident success of Rory's idea to provide qualitative as well as quantitative market research. Statistics, he had been convinced, did not supply an accurate enough picture. The reasons behind the statistics, why people did what they did, had to be known, as well. Apparently his theory had not only found many receptive ears, but had proven more accurate or effective in application than more traditional ways of collecting information.

Somehow that knowledge undermined Joanna's confidence as she approached the receptionist's desk.

Rory had grown far past the situation they had known and lived together. Not that such a factor should affect her purpose in any way, Joanna sternly told herself. She had simply come to see him. However, it might not be as easy as she had first thought, given this new set-up.

"Good morning." The receptionist looked at her with bright anticipation. She had the fresh young face of a woman barely out of her teens. Not someone with a lot of experience at fobbing off people, Joanna hoped.

"Good morning," she returned, projecting a completely at-ease smile to cover her inner tension. It was almost afternoon. It had seemed best to arrive just before twelve o'clock, giving Rory time to finish his meeting but ensuring he had not yet gone out for lunch. Now she had to ascertain if her timing was right. "I've come to see Mr. Grayson," she announced.

"Your name, please?" The receptionist glanced down at an appointment pad.

"I don't have an appointment. Is he free at the moment? It's a personal matter that won't take long."

This information earned a frown. "If you'll give me your name, I'll check with Mr. Grayson."

And that would be the end of that, Joanna thought grimly. Giving her name was too risky. "I have a better idea," she said, her eyes flashing with what she hoped looked like flirtatious mischief. "If you'll lend me your pad and pen, I'll write him a note and you can take it to him. I'm sure when he reads it he'll make time to see me."

The receptionist hesitated, clearly finding the suggestion irregular and the situation suspicious. Joanna confidently reached out for the items she'd asked for. Capitulation came after a few uncertain moments. As Joanna poised the pen to write, she could feel the young woman's eyes roving over her in intense speculation.

Her mind was rife with questions. What were the best words to provoke Rory's interest? Was the receptionist comparing her to some other woman in his personal life? Or—her heart clenched—his *wife*? Rory might have remarried. Why hadn't she thought of that? And why did she feel such a cramp of revulsion at such an idea? She didn't *care* what Rory did. He had killed her caring years ago.

An idea finally came to her, and she quickly wrote the words.

Success must feel sweet. Congratulations, Rory.

It was an objective comment, fair-minded, without rancour, hopefully ego-stroking enough to persuade Rory into seeing her for a moment or two. After all, the most sensible, rational thing to do was to expunge any lingering acrimony between them before moving on with their lives.

She added her signature, tore off the note page, folded it, handed it to the receptionist with a confident smile, put down the pen and turned aside as though considering sitting in one of the leather armchairs to wait.

She heard the receptionist leave the office. Nervous anticipation fluttered through Joanna's stomach. She forcefully assured herself it had nothing to do with

Rory or what he might think of her visit. It was perfectly natural to be on edge. The moment of truth and decision was at hand.

Now that she saw how well he had done for himself without her, Joanna was glad she had taken pains to look her best. Rory might scorn the superficiality of appearances, but Joanna didn't care about that. Pride demanded that he see she was doing fine by herself. More than that. Another man found her a very desirable asset to his life, and not just any other man, either. A highly eligible and discriminating one.

The sage-green knit suit she wore had border stripes of peach on the sleeves, the tunic and around the hem of the skirt. The effect was soft, feminine and elegant. The colour picked up the grey-green of her eyes, and she had matched the exact shade of sage in her high-heeled pumps and leather handbag.

She had spent an hour washing and blow-drying her long blonde hair so that it fell in soft waves around her shoulders, and her feathery fringe had a sweeping flyaway look on both sides of her face. Her make-up was faultless, a touch of silvery green on her eyelids, a grey pencil line to increase interest in the shape and width of her eyes, a subtle shading of blusher highlighting her cheekbones and a deeper shade of peach emphasising the sensual curves of her full-lipped mouth.

Although she was almost ten years older than when she had first met Rory, Joanna prided herself on having a dignity and sophistication that more than made up for any fresh-faced prettiness she might have lost. She had also regained her best weight. Rory could not fling the accusation of being anorexic at her now. The

firm roundness of her curves attested to her good
health and well-being.

Not that she had ever been truly anorexic. The
emotional stress of the divorce had simply robbed her
of any appetite. It was hard to enjoy food or anything
else when all one could feel was a soul-tearing sense of
failure. But she had survived and risen above all that.
If she could finally put Rory behind her today, she
could feel whole again, her own person, free to accept Brad as the man to share her future with.

Joanna swung around expectantly as she heard the
receptionist entering her office. The young woman
stood at her opened door, eyeing Joanna with blatant
curiosity as she said, "Mr. Grayson will see you now.
I'll take you to him."

"Thank you," Joanna replied, more loudly than
she meant to.

The prospect of facing Rory, now that it was upon
her, had an appalling effect. Her pulse leapt into a wild
beat that throbbed through her temples, making her
head feel like a buzz-saw. Her stomach could have
been a pancake being flipped over by a deft chef who
enjoyed showing off his dexterity. Her legs, as she
followed the receptionist, alternated between wooden
pegs and quivering jelly. It took a supreme act of will
to force her mind into reciting, *Rory means nothing to
me. Nothing, nothing, nothing.*

They walked the whole length of the cubicled area,
eyes looking up, assessing Joanna as she passed by.
Rory's office was in the corner at the far end, and it
was a relief to Joanna to reach it. The receptionist
ushered her inside. Joanna was vaguely aware of the

door being closed behind her, ensuring the privacy of the meeting, but the man in front of her claimed her attention with such devastating impact that she knew instantly she had been a fool to come.

"Joanna..." he said softly, as though he took pleasure in the sound of her name, not a trace of surprise in his voice or his eyes.

"Rory..." she managed to reply, her voice a bare, husky whisper.

He made no move towards her, gave no invitation for her to sit down and be at ease. Joanna was not really aware of the omission of standard politeness. She stared at him, and he stared right back at her in a silence that swirled with the painful bitterness of unfulfilled dreams and hopes and desires.

Joanna had never seen Rory like this, so elegantly dressed in a finely tailored three-piece suit, the sheen of some silk mixture in the cloth. Its subtle blue-grey colour and the blue and gold silk tie picked up the intense blueness of his eyes. His thick black hair had been stylishly layered to its natural waves, the riotous curls cut out of existence. It was a tamed image of the young man she had known and married, yet she sensed a self-assurance with it, an aura of control that was more dangerous than any overt rebellion against social standards.

This was a man who knew who he was, who used outer trappings to his advantage because it suited his purpose to be seen as a successful businessman. It had nothing to do with ego or status. The flash of cynicism in his eyes as he noted her surprise told Joanna that. Underneath his suit and haircut, he was still the

Rory who thought for himself, disdaining any influence by others.

Even his casual pose reflected that. If he'd wanted to impress her with his new affluence, he probably would have been sitting in the high-backed leather chair behind the expensive executive desk, but he was half sitting on the front edge of the desk, one leg stretched down to the floor, the other hitched up, dangling carelessly.

The hand resting on his raised thigh held her note. He lifted it, drawing her attention to what she had written.

"I can't believe you care whether or not I find success sweet. What do you want of me, Joanna?"

His mouth curved into a sensual little smile as his gaze dropped to rove down her body, making her uncomfortably aware of his intimate knowledge of it and the pleasure he had once taken in giving her pleasure. Her skin tingled as though he had caressed it, and her lungs stopped breathing as his eyes bored through the figure-hugging knit fabric, remembering the shape of her, the feel of her, all the secrets of her femininity that were no secret to him.

"You're wrong on both counts," she said quickly. "I *am* glad your ideas worked out so well. And I don't want anything of you, Rory."

His eyes lingered for a moment on the heave of her breasts before lifting to hers, a direct challenge in their vivid blueness. He raised one of his rakishly arched eyebrows, a mocking invitation for her to explain why she was here.

"I wanted to see you," she blurted out, her cheeks stinging with a rush of heat she could not control.

His mouth twisted with irony. "You thought the best way was to remind me of what you believed meant more to me than our marriage?"

She shook her head. "I didn't come to rake over old arguments."

"Does success make me sweeter for you, Joanna?"

"No." Her cheeks burnt even more fiercely at his insulting suggestion. "I'm not chasing after you, Rory."

He gave a harsh laugh. "Of course not. A woman of principle like yourself wouldn't bend that far. I was the one who did the chasing after you. It was you who showed me to your mother's door, demanding that I never darken it again."

He let the memory simmer between them before he added, "I simply find it intriguing that you now darken mine. Do you want the money you so proudly and bitterly refused from me then?"

The sting of this reminder evoked the passionate hatred of him she had felt that night. He had come with a cheque, offering her repayment of all the money it had cost her to support him while he was trying to make a go of his fledgling business. As though money could buy back her love after he had betrayed it with Bernice!

She glared at him with stormy eyes. "I didn't marry you for money and I didn't divorce you for money. I came to tell you I'm getting married to someone else."

She saw his jaw tighten, saw the taunting light fade from his eyes, leaving them empty of all expression.

There was a crackle of paper as his fingers crunched her note into a tight ball in his hand. He stood up, tall and straight and suddenly formidable in the clothes of his successful thrust into the world of commerce. He stepped around his desk and pointedly dropped the screwed-up paper into a bin. Then he faced her with a viciously mocking smile.

"So what can I do for you, Joanna? Write you a reference? To whom it may concern? I have known Joanna Harding intimately for a period of...now, how long was it, exactly? As I recall, you were nineteen when I—"

"Stop it, Rory!"

"Something wrong with my memory?"

"I don't need a reference." She lifted her chin in disdain of his demeaning summary of their time together. "Brad thinks I'm wonderful as I am."

"Brad..." He drawled the name as though measuring it for destruction. "Now where have I heard Brad before? Oh, yes! He was the wet-behind-the-ears hero in *The Rocky Horror Picture Show,* wasn't he?"

Joanna dragged in a deep breath to calm her churning insides. Her eyes flashed scorn at the cruel injustice of Rory's attitude. "I thought we could be civilised after all this time apart."

He laughed at her, his eyes glittering with primitive violence. "I have never felt civilised around you, Joanna."

"I thought we could let bygones be bygones," she persisted, clutching at dignity as a defence against the way his eyes were stripping her bare, reminding her of the wildness he had tapped in her sexuality, the mad mating they had once revelled in without any inhibitions.

"Can you forget what we had together?" he taunted.

"I wanted to wish you well, Rory," she forced out in determination to have done with this chaotically disturbing scene.

"How magnanimous of you! Is it better with Brad?"

The cheap shot goaded her into retaliating. "There's more to life than sex, Rory Grayson. It's a pity you haven't found that out. It means that whatever relationships you have will always fail."

His expression changed, a bleak fatigue drawing older lines on his face. "Wrong, Joanna," he said flatly. "I happen to be very good at relationships. Genuine relationships. Not ones that are screwed up by expectations that can't always be met when you want them met."

Shock turned into anger as Joanna digested Rory's perception of what had gone wrong in their marriage. He was blaming *her* for its failure, as though he hadn't contributed a hundredfold to the breakdown of any healing communication between them.

"Have you fathered any children I don't know about?" she fired at him with bitter venom. "Or do all your casual bed mates have convenient miscarriages?"

"Does your mother still ride a broomstick?" he shot back at her. "Force-feed you with poison pellets of hatred for me?"

"Leave my mother out of this!"

"Then leave my alleged affairs out, as well!"

"Right! Pardon me for mentioning them. They have long since ceased to be any of my business."

"Why don't you admit your real reason for coming, Joanna? Have a bit of self-honesty for once."

"I've already told you," she snapped.

He shook his head. "Hypocritical nonsense. You came to see if you were free of me. Because you weren't sure. And you had to know. A last throw of the dice before you married Brad. So let me clear your mind for you."

"How?" The word slipped out before she realised it was an admission.

Rory seized the opening, a look of dangerous devilment replacing the derisive challenge of a few moments ago. He started walking towards her, unshakeable purpose in every step. "A kiss for the bride-to-be," he said with a smile that torpedoed her stand of indifference to him.

"No." Her hand fluttered up to her throat as she frantically fought a rush of panic.

"A wish-you-well kiss from your ex-husband," Rory went on. "Make of it what you will, but kissed you certainly shall be."

She took a defensive step backwards.

"What have you to fear if you're free of me, Joanna?" he taunted. "Call it a gesture of final release. A graceful goodbye, demonstrating that bygones really are bygones and there's not a thing left between us. Not a jot. Not a speck. Not a molecule of feeling. Prove it to me that there's nothing left."

He was using her own words against her, all so irrefutably reasonable that it robbed her of any grounds to protest. She swallowed hard and came up with a burst of defiance. "I don't have to prove anything to you!"

"Then prove it to yourself."

He took the hand at her throat and placed it on his shoulder as he slid his other arm around her waist and scooped her hard against the long, lean power of his body. Joanna was shocked into passivity by a rush of warm feeling, a sense of rightness that seemed so treacherous she trembled in fear of what it meant. Long-standing familiarity, her mind screamed, fiercely rejecting any other cause for the sensation of being where she belonged.

Then his lips were on hers, gently grazing, not forcing any rough mastery over her, allowing her a choice of accepting his kiss or evading it. Rory had always been good at kissing, but his expertise in every act of love had aroused only hostility in her towards the end of their marriage. She told herself it was only curiosity that compelled her lips to move to the persuasive pressure of his, to open to the seductive caress of his tongue. She closed her eyes, needing to concentrate on examining the feelings he stirred now, to sort them out to her satisfaction, to prove...

All coherent thought was lost as Rory deepened the kiss, and Joanna's mind flooded with vibrant sensation. It was an invasion of all her deeply nursed defences against him, a shattering of bitterly held convictions, and it ignited a wild urge to make him experience the same inner turbulence.

Her mouth claimed his with a passionate intensity that sparked a response from him that spun them both out of any semblance of control. Her fingers dug into his hair, holding his head to hers. His hand splayed over the small of her back, arching her into intimate knowledge of the desire she was stirring.

A mad wave of exultation swept through Joanna. She wanted to goad him as he had goaded her, make him burn with the memories of all there had been between them, get under his skin in a way that defeated all the clever reasoning he could come up with.

She moved her body against his in deliberate incitement, recklessly uncaring of any consequences. An animal sound growled from his throat as he wrenched his mouth from hers. She opened her eyes to meet the raw blaze of searing questions in his, and whatever he read in them brought a heave of satisfaction and fast, decisive action.

He scooped Joanna off her feet and had her hugged against his chest in a whirl of male strength that left her gasping. He was heading for the door before she could collect her wits, then to compound the shock of what was happening the door opened and a woman stood there, gaping at them.

"You'll have to stand aside, Monique. You're in my way," Rory instructed.

Monique either defied him or was too stunned to obey. She was a gorgeous brunette, with a beautiful face framed by cascades of wild curls and a fantastic figure poured into a brilliant fuchsia suit. She was not the kind of woman who was used to being told to stand aside, Joanna thought, particularly by men. Her look of utter bewilderment caused Joanna's eyes to narrow suspiciously. Where did this woman fit into Rory's life?

It shocked Joanna to realise she felt as jealous of Rory as he must have felt about her with Brad. It had to be a hangover of possessiveness from their marriage. It couldn't have anything to do with loving.

"What are you doing?" the brunette finally found voice enough to ask.

"I'm abducting my ex-wife. Move aside and let us pass," came the firm command from Rory.

Monique backed out, looking dazedly at Joanna as Rory carried her from the office. "Your ex-wife," she repeated limply, then fired herself with purpose. "What about our dinner tomorrow night?"

"My apologies. There's no telling how long I'll be gone. Wife-napping is a time-consuming business," Rory tossed at her without the slightest hesitation as he set off striding past the row of computer cubicles.

Joanna felt a totally wanton sense of elation at this dismissal of the beautiful brunette's claims on him until she noticed the commotion Rory's progress was causing amongst his employees. Heads were popping up everywhere.

"Put me down," she commanded, taking swift stock of her position, which was extremely ambivalent, to say the least.

He ignored her and raised his voice to all those agog with interest. "One thing I want done while I'm away, and you can all get onto it. I want that Kawowski of Matchmakers Incorporated found and pinned down to a contract. We've never lost a customer yet, and we're not going to start now. Is that clear?''

There was a chorus of "yes, sir", while Joanna writhed between guilt and embarrassment. Impossible to admit to her fabrication about Mr. Kawowski in front of all these people, yet how could she let them waste so much time in looking for someone who didn't exist? The dilemma was too much for her to cope with, and in the overall picture it was a minor detail. They would soon find out there was no such person.

"Let me go, Rory!" she cried, trying to push out of his hold.

His arms tightened around her, clamping her against him. "You and I need to be together, Joanna."

"You can't kidnap me. You've got no right! I'm not your wife any more."

"The divorce was your idea, not mine."

"That's irrelevant. I won't let you carry me off. Call the police!" she demanded of the onlookers.

"Yes, call the police!" Rory agreed. "But give me half an hour's head start first. I'll give them a merry chase after that. If I can't get the story spread across the newspapers for all the world and Brad to read, my name's not Rory Grayson."

Joanna had sudden visions of Brad at his conference, with all his respected peers, being severely embarrassed by sensational tabloid stories about the woman he wanted to marry. "Don't call the police!" she yelled.

"You heard the lady. Don't call the police," Rory reiterated strongly.

She thumped him on the back in furious frustration. "You're ruining my life again."

"Well, we might as well be ruined together," he blithely replied. "That's only fair. Will someone please open the door for me and summon an elevator?"

With the way cleared ahead of him, he strode into the reception room with Joanna still in his captivity.

"Mr. Grayson!" the young woman behind the desk called after him, her voice on the edge of hysteria. She had never witnessed such a scene before and was totally lost as to how to act. She wrung her hands. "Your appointments, Mr. Grayson! What will I do?"

"Postpone them until further notice."

"But what will I say?"

"Say I'm off for the dirtiest weekend that any man could hope to have. That'll satisfy everybody."

He swept into the waiting elevator, pressed a button and grinned with wicked satisfaction as the doors slid shut.

CHAPTER THREE

As THE ELEVATOR hummed downwards, Joanna's mind reeled around Rory's outrageous presumption in hauling her off with him, the indignity he had subjected her to in doing so, the scandalous proof that he still didn't care what anybody thought of him and the terrible truth that she had instigated the whole chain of events by not freezing him off when he kissed her.

"This won't do you one bit of good, Rory Grayson!" she said in his ear, letting him know she was not about to fall under the spell of his wild and irrepressible nature again.

"It's done me a power of good already," he said cheerfully.

"I was only getting back at you with that kiss."

"If that was revenge, Joanna, I found it very sweet. The magic is still there for us. As strong as ever."

"I am *not* going to have a dirty weekend with you."

"Tell me about Brad, and why you're going to marry him."

The elevator doors rolled open and Rory strode into a basement garage while Joanna whirled through another bout of confusion. She should take pleasure in telling Rory how perfect Brad was for her, but she didn't want to. She no longer knew what she wanted.

Somehow Rory had turned everything upside down, including her.

At last he set her on her feet, and Joanna found herself standing beside the passenger door of a sage-green Jaguar, almost the exact colour of her suit. Rory liked green. Always had. But since when had he been able to afford such an expensive car?

Bemused by his sudden rise to wealth, Joanna did not think of trying a getaway. Rory unlocked the door and opened it before she realised he wasn't holding her captive anymore. He stood back from her, one hand on the door, the other gesturing an open invitation to choose her own course. He spoke quietly, seriously, his whole manner in marked contrast to all that had gone before.

"You may find this difficult to believe, Joanna, but I want you to be happy. I thought I was the man you could best be happy with. Even when things were wrong between us, I still felt we were right for each other, right in a way that I've never felt with anyone else."

He paused, searching her eyes for a similar admission, some hint of vulnerability to what he was saying, but Joanna stubbornly resisted giving him any concession. If she gave Rory an inch he would take a mile. Yet his words did strike a deeply buried chord in her heart. She had believed that, too. Until he betrayed her faith in the worst possible way.

He gave her a wry smile. "I can't go back and do things differently. If I'm not the man you can be happy with, then I want to know that Brad is. So long as I know you'll be happy with him, Joanna, I can let bygones be bygones. But if you're not sure about marrying him..."

"I didn't say that," she cut in swiftly, defensively.

"Joanna, there's no engagement ring on your finger."

Her eyes flashed defiance of this superficial judgement. "You didn't give me a ring."

"In those days I couldn't afford what I wanted to give you. Is that the case with Brad?"

She grimaced in vexation at being pinned down. "He's away at the moment. When he comes back..."

"So this is decision time. And you came to me for help."

"No, I didn't."

"Joanna." He reached out and took her hand, his long, lean fingers curling around hers, stroking them, lightly pressing their persuasion. "Remember how we used to talk? Tell each other everything? No holding back?"

"That was before," she protested, her eyes flashing with the pain he had given her. Yet she didn't tug her hand out of his. Somehow it triggered good memories, of when her love for Rory had been young and innocent and full of joy.

"I have no wish to rake over old arguments, either," he said softly. "We'll talk about the future. Your future. How you want it to be. How you see it with Brad. As you say, you don't have to prove anything to me, Joanna, but come with me now and prove whatever you need to prove to yourself. Conclusively. That is what you want, isn't it?"

She stared at their linked hands, feeling his warmth and his strength and desperately wanting what he was offering. Could she trust him to do what he said? She lifted her gaze, meeting his in fearful uncertainty. "You'll let me go free whenever I want to, Rory?"

"Whenever you want to," he promised, the steady blaze of his blue eyes giving her the assurance she needed.

She heaved a sigh to relieve her pent-up turmoil. The voice of hard-learnt cynicism told her it was still a risk to go with him. He undoubtedly meant to take advantage of her compliance, one way or another. Nevertheless, he had to know that force wouldn't get him any lasting advantage. He had already changed tack on that score. So what harm could it do to spend an hour or two with him? If it clarified her feelings, it would be time well spent.

"All right. I'll come with you. For a while," she said warily.

He smiled, a happy, lilting smile that transmitted unbounded joy, the kind of smile Rory used to give her long ago, enveloping her in his pleasure. Joanna's heart gave a kick, sending a tingle of excited anticipation through her veins as she stepped into his car and settled herself into the low-slung passenger seat. Rory closed the door and moved quickly around to the driver's side, as though he could not contain an eager exhilaration at the prospect of being with her again.

Joanna deliberately kept her gaze averted from him as he settled himself in the seat beside her. How she could find him so compellingly attractive was deeply worrying. Reawakened sexual chemistry. That's all it could be. The years apart had somehow corroded the hurts that had formed a protective shield around her.

She had proved she could live without Rory, although *existing* was probably the more accurate word to describe most of her life since she had left him. Nevertheless, it was paramount she remember these dangerously wayward feelings couldn't be trusted. It was time she concentrated on the problem that had brought her here, whether or not she could ever give herself wholeheartedly to Brad.

Her head told her Brad Latham was a good, dependable man who would never give her the terrible pain that Rory had. She liked him very much. They had a lot of interests in common. And while liking wasn't love, Joanna didn't trust love anymore. Love could lead one badly astray.

But what about sharing Brad's bed for the rest of her life? Sex with him was pleasant enough. Fine, really. She had honestly believed she would never feel passionate desire again, yet Rory still aroused it, throwing all her sensible reasoning into chaos. If she married Brad, would she always be haunted with memories of what lovemaking had been like with Rory?

She probably shouldn't be using Rory as some kind of yardstick. To Rory, sex was one of the pleasures in life to be enjoyed whenever and wherever the urge occurred. And the urge had occurred once too often, Joanna savagely reminded herself. At the wrong time, in the wrong place and with the wrong woman. One thing she *was* certain of in her own mind—Brad would never be unfaithful to her.

The powerful engine of the sports car throbbed into life. Joanna watched Rory's hands slide around the steering wheel as he directed the Jaguar out of the garage and onto the road. He obviously enjoyed the feel of power under his touch. He was a tactile person, sensitive to the tiniest vibration, attuned to responding to it. Joanna wondered if Monique knew that.

"So tell me about Brad. What's he like? Handsome? Physically attractive?"

"Yes."

Not in the same traffic-stopping class as Monique, but Joanna was not about to tell Rory that. Besides, Brad *was* handsome. While his strong, clean-cut features had none of the rakish charm of Rory's more dramatic individuality, nor the mischievous twinkle in his eyes, he was certainly good-looking. Everyone thought so.

"That's not very forthcoming, Joanna," Rory chided. "Tell me what he's like."

"He's not a taker like you," she shot at him in a burst of resentment. "He gives a lot of himself. He cares about people."

"A sterling character," Rory drawled. "What does he do for a living?"

"He's the headmaster of—"

"Oh, no, no, no!" Rory rolled his eyes at her. "Don't tell me this is true. Not a headmaster. Not after me. Headmasters are dull, conventional people."

"Brad is not dull. He's a go-getter and very progressive. Which is why he's the headmaster of a prestigious private school."

"Worse!" Rory groaned. "How could you even think of throwing your lot in with a stuffy, narrow-minded, elitist snob of the worst kind? To go from me to such a man..." He shook his head. "It's not only insulting to me, it belittles you."

"Stop the car and let me out," Joanna commanded tersely.

"Not on this downbeat note. We haven't got to where we're going to yet."

"I'm not having you criticising someone you don't know anything about."

"Put it down as a minor outburst of irritation and annoyance." He threw her a smile of apologetic appeal. "I simply can't bear to think of you putting yourself into a straitjacket for the rest of your life. That might suit your mother, Joanna, but—"

"I thought we agreed to leave my mother out of this."

"You told me you didn't want to live like your mother, always thinking of what others think of you." He cast her a look of concern. "That's how you'd have to be, married to the headmaster of a private school, Joanna. No putting a foot wrong. No letting your hair down. Dressed to the nines all the time. Like Caesar's wife. Beyond reproach."

"Better than being Nero's wife, not knowing whose bed he was coming from," she sniped.

Rory sighed deeply. "Now is that being reasonable, hitting me below the belt, unfairly, I might add, when I'm doing my best to be helpful? What happened to bygones being bygones?"

"You brought my mother into it."

"Hard to keep her out of it when she must be promoting this match as though it was made in heaven," came the dry reply.

In all honesty, Joanna could not deny that. She bit her lips and brooded for a few moments before her mind retrieved the claim by Rory that she had hit him below the belt *unfairly* with her shot about adultery. Was he still trying to deny what he'd done? While she couldn't prove he had been unfaithful with more than one woman, one was quite enough for Joanna.

What had hurt most at that killing moment of revelation was that she herself had been trying to get pregnant for months. Not that Rory had known that. He had wanted to wait until they were financially on their feet before starting a family. Having a baby had been her decision, a desperate bid to rekindle the intimacy they had lost in endless arguments about what they should be doing and where they should be heading. For Rory to have had sex with another woman and impregnate her was a double betrayal.

Joanna could never forgive it. And she wasn't about to forget it, either, no matter what Rory said, or did, or how he made her feel. Time did not mitigate some offences. Rory might be able to prove that Brad was the wrong man for her, but that didn't make him the right one.

Her attention was caught by the view of beach and sea as the car turned into a street that led to them. "Where are we?" she asked, realising she had taken no notice of direction from the time they had left the office building in Chatswood.

"Dee Why," Rory answered.

It was one of a string of beaches running north from the head of Sydney Harbour, but that was as much as Joanna knew about Dee Why. She had never been here.

"This is where I live now," Rory added, turning the car into a driveway lined with palm trees and artistic clumps of other tropical plants. It led to a row of private garages, separated by white brick archways.

Expensive architecture. Expensive landscaping. It fitted with the expensive car, yet Joanna had difficulty in coming to terms with this new image of Rory. "You're taking me to your home?" she questioned sharply, struggling to accept the evidence that Rory could now afford the luxury of living in what was clearly a block of very expensive apartments.

"I'd like you to see it."

He threw her a grin that somehow reflected the intimate understanding they had once shared. Joanna's heart did a treacherous jig. While she was still berating herself for being ridiculously affected by what could only be a memory, Rory parked the car and alighted.

Joanna sat in a feverish quandary as he walked around to the passenger side. She had serious doubts about the wisdom of being alone with Rory in his home. The more sensible course was to demand they go somewhere else. Considering the effect of Rory's grin on her, probably the *most* sensible course was to leave him right now before he managed to confuse and disturb her any further with the powerful attraction he evoked with increasing ease.

Yet an irresistible tug of curiosity undermined all common sense. She wanted to know how Rory lived now. When he opened her door, Joanna found herself stepping out and saying nothing.

Rory led her into a grand foyer where there were elevators and a staircase. The patterned mosaic of tiles on the floor had the stamp of class. A fountain streaming over an artistic arrangement of modern sculptures made its statement, as well. Wherever Joanna looked, money, and lots of it, screamed at her.

Rory smiled as he ushered her into an elevator, his blue eyes dancing wickedly with the memory of their last elevator ride.

"Don't try it," she warned.

"Perish the thought."

He pressed a button and linked his hands behind his back in an unholy demonstration of harmless innocence, while the smile stretched into an irrepressible and madly tantalising grin.

If he thought these accoutrements of wealth were going to change her opinion of him, he could think again, Joanna determined in bitter resolve. Money was not going to change one thing between them. It hadn't swayed her judgement in the past and it wasn't going to sway it now. Only the person counted, not what he or she had in material possessions.

Nevertheless, as they rode up to the top floor, Joanna had the uneasy realisation she felt more acutely alive than she had for a very long time. It was as though every nerve in her body was tingling with awareness, and every sense was tuned to the vitality emanating from her ex-husband.

It made her ask herself why she never felt like this with Brad. The answer came all too swiftly. Brad was safe and completely predictable. Almost boringly predictable. Rory might be many things, but he had never, ever, been boring. He provoked extremes of feeling as naturally as he breathed.

What she had to keep reminding herself was that many of those extremes were bad, so bad that in the end she couldn't live with them. And that was why Brad was better for her. There was probably a penalty for every choice one made in life, Joanna decided, and boring was definitely easier to live with than bad. At least she always knew where she was with Brad Latham.

Despite this furious reasoning, the rest of Joanna did not demonstrate any sense of conviction. Both physically and emotionally she was experiencing an alarmingly high degree of anticipation, which heightened further when Rory led her out of the elevator and into his apartment. Was she such a foolish masochist she enjoyed putting herself in danger with Rory Grayson? Joanna wondered.

Her feet stopped dead at the entrance to Rory's living room, and all the churning mental activity came to an abrupt end. In front of her was the re-creation of the picture she had once cut out of the *Home Beautiful* magazine, the picture she had shown Rory as her ideal dream living room. And it was all here, perfect in every detail, stunningly mind-blowing in its fantastic reality.

The cedar ceiling, glazed Chinese sandstone on the floor, terracotta leather lounges, white walls, Aboriginal paintings, Persian rugs, wonderful pots and urns with magnificent ferns spilling over them, a dining table of gleaming cedar, and the leather upholstered Italian chairs she had so admired, all of it flooded with light from huge expanses of glass facing the sea. Doors led out to a covered terrace where brightly cushioned cane furniture was set amongst potted palms and more greenery climbing around the archways that framed the view.

Nothing had been missed.

But how had Rory remembered it?

Had he kept the picture?

If so, why?

And why breathe life into *her* dream when it couldn't mean anything anymore?

CHAPTER FOUR

"Did I get it right, Joanna?"

The soft question shivered through her. It was as though Rory was walking over the grave of their marriage, bringing it to life again. But it was dead. Dead! And Joanna didn't know if it was terrible or wonderful, seeing this ghost of it in the fulfilment of one of her dreams.

She couldn't look at him. She fought for a facade of indifference as she numbly accepted the glass of champagne he offered her. Her mind dazedly registered the fact he must have left her side to open a bottle, but she hadn't been aware of it.

How much time had passed since her feet had faltered to a shocked halt? And why was Rory giving her champagne? Did he think he had cause to celebrate? Was he enjoying some ultimate sense of revenge in showing her that he now had what she had wanted?

"This must have cost you a fortune," she said in a brittle voice, limply waving an arm to encompass the furnishings.

"The result was worth it, don't you think?" he replied, still with that low throb of disturbing intimacy in his tone.

Joanna deliberately evaded giving a response, wary of revealing what she was feeling. Instead she asked, "How did you make so much money so quickly, Rory? It's only been three years."

"It's because I can draw maps. Important maps. Or at least my computers can."

"Maps?" Joanna frowned her bewilderment. "How is that connected to your market research?"

"With my demographic data bases, showing people's requirements, I can demonstrate the most viable and strategic location where any business should be," Rory answered matter-of-factly. "Do you realise how important it can be for a business to have that information?"

"Yes, but I still don't understand how you could earn so much in so little time," Joanna demurred, drawn into looking at him by his apparently blasé attitude towards his success.

His eyes gently derided the puzzlement in hers. "It's not the time I spend on a job that's important, Joanna. It's the knowledge I have. A large corporation will spend half to a million dollars without blinking to access that data. It can mean the difference between failure and success. And I have a stranglehold on this market. I was the first into it, and no-one has been able to catch me."

"So all the spadework paid off in the end," she commented dryly.

His mouth twisted into a travesty of a smile. "Ironic, isn't it? When we were married and together it was a struggle for me to survive in business from week to week. You had to support me. After you left me, it started to roll in in the millions, month after month."

The open reference to their marriage stirred conflicting emotions. Joanna sought to hide them by lifting her glass of champagne in a toast to his achievements. "Congratulations, Rory. You've certainly done well for yourself."

His eyes mocked the distance she was trying to keep between them. "Perhaps you did me a good service in walking out on me, Joanna. It concentrated my mind on making a success of something."

"It must give you a lot of satisfaction," she retorted lightly.

He lifted his glass and sipped the champagne before pointedly remarking, "Funny thing about money. When you don't have it, you think it's the answer to everything. When you've got more than you could ever possibly need, you find out there's still something missing."

Did he mean her?

She tore her gaze from the intense provocation in his and forced her legs to walk casually through the room. "But you must enjoy what you have here," she said, indirectly seeking some clue to his feelings.

"Yes," he answered, too briefly to reveal anything. He strolled past her, heading for a set of doors that led onto the terrace outside. "Sorry it's such a grey day," he tossed over his shoulder. "Normally this room is flooded with sunshine."

To Joanna, it was a taunting reminder of what she had hated most about the apartment they had rented to keep living expenses to a minimum. The windows had been small and facing the wrong direction for any ray of sunshine to warm or cheer the place. She had stipulated to Rory that when they could afford to buy a home of their own, it had to have rooms with lots of sunshine coming in, and if possible, a view of...

"The view of the sea is better from out here," he said, finishing her thought for her and gesturing an invitation to accompany him onto the terrace.

Joanna walked forward like an automaton, drawn almost against her will to see all there was to see, despite the inner torment it aroused. From the railing between the arches, there was a magnificent view of the sea and a long wide sweep of beach, as well. On a sunny day it would be glorious. Even now, with the sky overcast and threatening rain, it was still perfect to Joanna, precisely what she had dreamed of having.

"Geraniums," Rory said, pointing to the ceramic pots near the railing. "Since it's midwinter they're not in flower right now, but that one over there is red, that one a sort of apricot, that one..."

He listed off the geraniums she had envisioned as adding to the Mediterranean look she'd favoured. How he had memorised them she did not know, but he had forgotten nothing. Then, as though he could command nature itself to do his bidding, the clouds parted and the sun beamed a brief benevolence on both of them. It was always like that with Rory, Joanna thought. The most surprising, unexpected and improbable things happened.

Again he gave her that heart-kicking smile, sharing a moment made specially for them, or so it seemed.

Joanna was somehow incapable of resisting when he took her hand, enfolding it warmly in his. He drew her along the terrace, beyond the living room, past a cane and glass table setting that was positioned outside a curtained room, to the end of the last archway, where there was a rich profusion of potted palms and hanging baskets of ferns.

Then Rory showed her it wasn't the last archway at all. There was another that was glassed in on three sides, and inside this part of the terrace was an even more mind-wrenching sight. The whole space was taken up by a huge spa bath, luxuriously set in richly veined green onyx with gold taps and crystal jars of bath oils around the wide ledges.

"To make you feel relaxed and pampered," Rory murmured.

After we make love. That's what she had said, imagining the jets of the spa shooting tingly bubbles over their sensitised flesh while they moved their bodies sensuously together in the scented flow of the bath.

"You can lie back and be soothed by the sight of tropical greenery, or watch the sea," Rory continued softly. "At night you can see the stars. There are skylights specially built above the bath so you can look up and see the universe revolve if you want to stay there long enough."

That was what he had added when she had described what would be heavenly to her. She remembered laughing in delight but never dreaming it could really be possible for them. A delicious fantasy, totally unrealistic, yet Rory had made it come true.

Tears pricked her eyes as an ungovernable well of emotion surged from her heart. It wasn't fair, her mind cried. How could Rory do this when everything was over between them? As though in tune with the ache gathering inside her, there was a roll of thunder and the sunshine blinked out. Heavy drops of rain began to fall.

Rory released her hand and quickly stepped over to the set of glass doors leading to the curtained room. He unlocked them, stepped inside, summoned her to follow him. While she hesitated, reluctant to be subjected to more tormenting remembrances, the curtains swished open, trapping Joanna with the worst revelation of all.

She felt like a sleepwalker compelled by forces beyond her control, as her feet took her over the threshold of the last and grandest dream. She now knew what the cane table setting was for. Breakfast on the terrace outside the master bedroom.

Inside was the private white leather lounge setting with the glass coffee table resting on a polished block of granite. Beneath her feet was a thick, sumptuous carpet in the palest of pale greens, inviting her to take her shoes off and sink her toes into it. She didn't have to look to know there was a doorway to her right, opening to a passage to the spa bath. Her gaze inevitably drifted to the king-size bed at the far end of the room. The far, far end. The room itself was king-size, luxurious space enough to give each piece of furniture a stylish placement.

The quilt on the bed was a swirl of lilac and white and pale green and duck-egg blue. A pile of silk cushions picked up the colours, and above the padded headboard hung a huge, exquisite painting of water-lilies. On either side of the bed were polished granite and glass tables, holding elegant lamps, their gleaming porcelain bases in delicate lilac, their shades fluted silk in palest green.

Along the side walls were wonderful watercolours of birds, and some magnificent Lladro figurines were featured on pedestals. If she had chosen them herself, Joanna knew she could not have chosen better. She had the sick, hollow feeling that Rory had picked them out of her mind with unerring precision.

She turned to him with haunted, anguished eyes, unable to pretend indifference any longer. It didn't matter that she found him watching her, waiting for her reaction. The need for truth tore at her heart.

"Why, Rory? Why did you do this?"

He gave a harsh little laugh. "It seemed like a good idea at the time."

Which, of course, was no answer at all.

Joanna didn't realise her hand was shaking until champagne started dribbling over her fingers. She stared in dismay as Rory took the glass from her. He deposited both their glasses on the coffee-table. It was easy for him to be calm and complacent, she thought resentfully. He wasn't being turned inside out by what he had been living with day after day.

"What was your intention when you set out to turn my dreams into reality?" she hurled at him. "Did you think you could use it to persuade me into coming back to you?"

"Don't be a fool, Joanna." He straightened up, his eyes glittering hard mockery as he withdrew a handkerchief from his coat pocket and strolled to her. "The night you threw me out of your mother's house and said you never wanted to see me again, I took your words quite literally," he drawled. "I would never have chased after you a second time. Never tried to persuade you differently."

"Then give me an explanation of why..."

Words choked in her throat as he took her hand and began wiping the sticky wetness from her fingers. As though he hadn't already smashed every defence she had against him, the familiar intimacy of such a service made Joanna more tremulous. She swallowed hard and forced her voice to work. It produced a burst of harsh bitterness.

"Why did you give life and substance to a dream that was dead and buried?"

His eyes flashed up and seared hers with the vivid intensity of their challenge. "If I gave it life and substance, it's not dead. It never will be dead, as far as I'm concerned. And it's not dead for you, either, Joanna, however deeply you might want to bury it."

Joanna stood like a mesmerised rabbit, feeling the unrelenting purpose flowing from him, knowing he was going to kiss her again, kiss her until he ripped away all her inhibitions and forced the admission he wanted to hear, driving her beyond the bounds of reason with the wild heat of passion that only Rory had ever drawn from her.

She knew she shouldn't let him, so why was there a mad craving in her mind to experience it once more?

One last time? Why didn't she move away when he removed his suit jacket and tossed it onto the closest armchair? Why did her ears only hear the chaotic drumming of her heart as he began unbuttoning his waistcoat?

She watched his fingers deftly complete their task, and felt her body yearning for their touch, felt the warm tingle of anticipation spreading down from her stomach. Her lungs tightened as his silk tie joined the other discarded clothes on the chair, and she was conscious of her breasts rising and falling with her urgent gasps for air.

Somewhere a thread of sanity screamed, *I've got to stop this now. Before he starts. Before it's too late.* It stirred her conscience. *Remember Brad,* it shrieked.

Where the strength came from she did not know. Her legs felt hopelessly feeble, but she forced herself to turn and walk to the glass doors, telling herself she would be safe outside the bedroom. She needed the sea wind in her face, cold air to clear her mind of the feverish wanting that shouldn't be there.

The door slid open easily but somehow her fingers stuck to the handle, clutching it as though it could pour more strength into the purpose of getting away from the temptation behind her. But the sound of the sea rushed into her ears like a siren's song, surging beneath the storm of stinging rain, a rhythmic roar that found its echo inside her as Rory's hands slid up to claim her breasts and press her body to the hard, virile warmth of his.

Did he make her sway, or was it some wanton desire in her that found intense satisfaction in the roll of her bottom against the taut muscularity of his thighs? It felt so good she couldn't help savouring the sensation for a moment. Then his cheek brushed her hair away from her ear, and his mouth moved slowly, hotly, sensuously down her throat, and her head leaned back, offering more access before she realised what she was doing.

"No..." she moaned, guilt forcing a protest through a thick tide of lassitude that dragged at her will, pleading for a stay of judgement, for another trial, for another result that would wipe away the past and give her back the future she had once dreamed of.

Rory either didn't hear or took no notice. He dropped a hand to her stomach, began a rotating caress that made all her nerve ends leap in excitement at the intimacy it promised. She felt the hardening thrust of his manhood pressing against her, felt a rush of liquid warmth, the pulsating response of her body to the urgency coming from his.

As her legs started to quiver, the shock of her dreadful loss of control propelled Joanna into desperate action. This was wrong. Had to be wrong. She jerked her head forward, clawed at Rory's hands, staggered out of his embrace, plunging onto the terrace and bumping into one of the cane chairs.

"I don't want—"

"You do!"

He spun her around to face him. His eyes blazed with a need stripped raw by the compliance she had already given. He followed her agitated step backwards, scooped her into his arms again, and his mouth silenced any more words she might have spoken.

He was right. She wanted him to the deepest core of her being, and to hell with whether it was wrong or not! Her tongue duelled with his in a passionate drive for appeasement of the desire churning through her. Her arms wound around his neck. Her body writhed against his, released from all restraint by the explosion of need that demanded satisfaction.

A reckless excitement pumped through her veins as she felt his hands push down her thighs and gather up her skirt. *Yes*, she thought fiercely. *Do it! Do it!* He pressed her back against the breakfast table. Cold air swirled against her legs as he removed her panties.

Then she was on the table and he was inside her, a hot surge of flesh that eased the craving with its plunging fullness. Her muscles convulsed around him in ecstatic pleasure. He lowered her onto the tabletop, leaning over her, kissing her mouth, her throat, his hands sliding under her pullover, gliding over her silk camisole, gathering up her breasts, kneading them, eyes glittering into hers, feasting on her response to each inward stroke of their mutual possession.

Joanna wrapped her legs around his waist, her own eyes gloating over his driven expression, the need, the want, the strain for ultimate fulfilment with her. Spits of rain blew over them. Wind streaked through their hair. Thunder and lightning lent an even more primitive ferocity to their coupling. The sea pounded a louder heartbeat than before, and to Joanna's ears it thrummed one word—Rory, Rory, Rory.

Her body arched in a paroxysm of pleasure as one climax spilled into another, sweetly melding together for an exquisite space of time out of time. Yesterday was a forgotten memory. Tomorrow remained in limbo. Only now existed, a now of Rory and her together again as it always should have been.

Then he gathered her into his arms and carried her inside to the bed he had bought for them, and what did it matter now to undress and be completely naked with him, to enjoy the feel of each other, to revel in the intimacy of uninhibited sensuality?

He was beautiful. So essentially male in his athletic build. Hard muscle and firm flesh and smooth skin, and hands that knew how to touch, and a mouth that knew how to weave every erotic magic there could be between a man and a woman. How could she deny herself what Rory could give her? She had missed this so much. She knew the wordless harmony she was feeling with him couldn't last, but she didn't have to think about that. Not yet.

CHAPTER FIVE

THE BATH WAS HEAVENLY, better than Joanna had imagined. Her body was deliciously bombarded with streams of bubbling water. Scented froth kept bouncing up and tickling her face. It was fun. It was decadent. It was sinful with Rory lounging low in the bath at the other end, watching her enjoyment with eyes that danced wicked satisfaction.

"Stay the weekend with me, Joanna," he said softly, one foot stroking its persuasion down the calf of her leg.

"So you can have the dirtiest weekend any man could hope to have?" she mocked, wary of extending this crazy involvement with Rory. She didn't want it to stop. She wanted Rory to keep loving her. But she knew if she started loving him back she would again be vulnerable to the worst kind of hurt.

He grinned unashamedly. "I'd give you the dirtiest weekend any woman could hope to have."

That was undoubtedly true. His toes played with hers, reminding her of the kind of lovemaking that had laughter as an ingredient. Sex was always serious business with Brad.

Her mind swiftly shied away from the guilt that thought stirred. She wasn't committed to Brad. Nor had she meant this to happen with Rory. Now that it had, she knew she could never be Brad's wife. That, at least, was clear.

"All right. One weekend," she decided with a heady sense of recklessness. "I'll give it a try, Rory, but I walk out the moment I stop liking it."

"Of course. You're free to do whatever you want, Joanna. You always have been," he reminded her, his eyes glinting their knowledge of how much she had liked the hours of intimacy they had already shared.

Spending the weekend with him, however, did pose problems. The afternoon was almost gone. Her mother was probably already home from Jessica's and would undoubtedly wait for Joanna's return before preparing dinner. Joanna couldn't simply disappear without explanation.

"I'll have to call my mother," she said on a note of rueful resignation, knowing full well it would raise complications she would rather do without.

Rory raised a mocking eyebrow. "You need her permission? How old are you, Joanna? Twenty-nine? Almost thirty?"

"Don't be ridiculous, Rory. It's a courtesy. She might think I've had an accident."

"Well, we wouldn't want to worry your mother, would we?" he drawled, his mouth curling sardonically. "There's a phone on the wall beside you. Call her now."

His eyes challenged her to demonstrate how free and independent she was. It recalled the bitter words he had hurled at her when she had walked out of their marriage. *Sure! Run home to Mummy! Be her precious daughter again! Let her know she won after all!*

He had been wrong then and he was wrong now. Joanna couldn't let it pass. "I'd like to get this straight, Rory. I don't know what bee you've got in your bonnet about my mother, but you might remember that I chose to marry you and be estranged from her most of the time we were married," she said quietly.

"I remember, Joanna." His eyes were still hard. "I remember how much it hurt you. I remember how you wept when she forced the choice upon you. It wasn't your choice."

"I wept because she hated you more than she loved me. I guess every girl dreams of the wedding she'll have one day. And every mother dreams of her daughter's wedding. When my mother denied me that, it was like she was denying me as her daughter. Of course, it hurt."

"But you went back to her, Joanna. And that was more than a denial of me," he pointed out in a calm, dispassionate voice. "Your mother was always my enemy. You didn't move to neutral ground when you walked out on me and our marriage. You went to your mother's side."

"It didn't matter where I went, Rory. What we had was dead for me then. My mother was ill and she needed help."

"Would she have come to you if you were ill and needed help?"

"I don't know. I would hope so. In any event, I'm not my mother. I do what I think is right."

"Yes." His mouth curled into an ironic smile. "I'll grant you that, Joanna. Your sense of rightness is an enormous strength. I admire you for it. Always have. But it's also a weakness in making you blind to other things."

"What other things?"

"Not everything's black and white."

If he was referring to his affair with Bernice, Rory could talk himself blue in the face, and Joanna would still never be able to excuse it.

Perhaps he saw the rejection in her eyes. He quickly turned the conversation away. "Why have you stayed with your mother all this time? You have nothing in common."

She wanted to say that grief made everything else meaningless, and her grief over the death of their marriage had never really ended. But she wasn't ready to reveal that truth yet. Perhaps later, when she felt more secure about Rory's feelings for her.

"I guess there's still a blood tie that gives a sense of belonging, and I needed to belong somewhere," she replied. "As for my mother feeding me poison pellets of hatred for you, you're absolutely wrong about that, Rory. I made a rule that we never talk about you."

"In that case, you'll want to hide the fact you're with me now," he deduced sardonically.

"What I do with my life is my own business."

"Then go ahead and call your mother. As a courtesy."

Joanna reached out, unhooked the telephone from the wall and jabbed out the numbers. She glared determination at Rory, whose sardonic smile challenged

it. There could be no evasion about telling her mother
the truth. Rory would not respect her or anything
she'd said if she prevaricated.

"It's Joanna," she started.

"Thank heaven! I've been worried out of my
mind!" her mother cried.

This startled Joanna into another line of thinking.
"What about?" she demanded, her mind instantly
leaping to some urgent problem with her sister or
nieces.

"Have you got away from *that man?*" Pure venom
speared through her mother's voice.

Joanna's initial shock did not last long. She could
feel herself tensing up with anger. How her mother
knew about Rory she could not imagine, but only he
had ever drawn forth that tone of hatred. She forced
herself to sound calm and unemotional.

"What man, Mum?"

"You know perfectly well what man, Joanna,"
came the impatient and condemning snipe. "Tennis
finished early for Jessica because of the rain, and
when I came home, Poppy Dalton called to ask if
you'd like to spend the evening with her. Then I saw
the telephone book open with Rory Grayson's business number circled."

Joanna privately cursed herself. Her mother had
obviously pounced on it like a bloodhound. Now the
bounds of discretion were cracked wide open, and
raging disapproval was rampant.

"What on earth possessed you to see him again?"
she ranted on. "Have you no sense of propriety,
Joanna? What do you expect Brad to think? To put

yourself into such a position as to let *that man* abduct you—"

"How did you know that, Mum?" Joanna cut in tersely.

"I rang his office and that was what I was told. Whoever answered was as bold as brass about it. Titillated by his outrageous behaviour, no doubt. I can only think his whole staff is as disgusting as he is."

"What right do you think you have to poke into my private and personal business?" Joanna demanded, feeling a well of outrage that her mother should check up on what she was doing.

"It was for your own good," she blustered. "*That man* turns your head, Joanna. You need to be protected from him."

"I'll make my own decisions about what I need, Mum, and I'll thank you to stay out of my affairs." The coldness with which Joanna delivered these words effectively silenced her mother, at least for a few moments. "Now if I can have your attention, I was calling to say—"

"You're still with him, aren't you?" her mother burst out in bitter frustration.

"Yes," Joanna stated bluntly. "And I'll stay with him as long as I like. So don't expect me home until you see me."

"What about Brad?"

"That's *my* business, too, Mum."

Joanna hung up the telephone with the fire of rebellion burning in her belly. Her eyes flashed at Rory, daring him to make any demeaning comment on the conversation. The taunting smile was gone. His expression held a weighing consideration, as though she had surprised him in some way and he was calculating what it meant.

"Satisfied?" she tossed at him.

"Are you?" he returned softly, aware of her seething emotions and careful not to draw any wrath onto his head.

She realised he was leaving her to assess her mother's behaviour in relation to both her own life and her association with him. The word *freedom* sizzled through her mind. It was what Rory had once represented to her. And still did. Freedom from all the narrow confines of what her mother considered proper. Freedom of self-expression. Freedom to be anything she wanted, do anything she wanted.

By being the person he was, Rory fed the rebellion Joanna had buried for the three years they had been apart. Giving it life again was dangerous. It could lead to terrible hurt. But it made her feel brilliantly alive.

Which led her to wonder how much of her real self she had buried along with her rebellion. Perhaps Rory was right in claiming they were right for each other. They certainly seemed to be as lovers. But she couldn't commit herself wholeheartedly to him ever again. That was definitely out. On the other hand, being lovers . . . and friends . . . was that possible?

"As I said, I'll chance this weekend with you, Rory." Her mouth curved into a wry smile. "And live with the consequences."

His smile approved her daring and invited more. "So why don't you come up this end and say hello?"

Laughter gurgled from her throat. For this weekend, her mother and Brad could live on some other planet. She moved through the water slowly, provocatively, blowing gusts of bubbles at Rory, uncaring of anything but the mischievous laughter in his twinkling blue eyes.

"How many times a day do you have to make love, Rory Grayson?" she teased, brushing her breasts lightly up his chest.

"Oh, I have about a thousand days and nights to make up for," he answered blithely.

Which more or less added up to the three years they had spent apart. Joanna settled on his lap and playfully lathered his hair. "Are you saying that you missed me?"

"I missed the good times."

It was a sobering reminder that nothing had been resolved between them. Joanna wondered if that was all he wanted from her now, a good time. Perhaps he wanted this weekend to wash her out of his hair, once and for all. Yet if that was so, why had he built so much of her into his home?

Then he started stroking her back, and she decided thinking was not conducive to full enjoyment of what Rory did so well. For the moment, all she wanted to do was feel and live the good times once more.

The storm had long since passed over, and the early winter night was clear enough to show a few stars before Rory suggested their energy level could do with some boosting. "How does Italian food appeal to you?" he asked, knowing it was her favourite.

"Mmm. Minestrone. Lasagne. Cassata." It was what she had always ordered in the old days whenever they allowed themselves a night out.

He laughed. "You don't have to count the cost tonight, Joanna. Whatever you want."

"You can wave a magic wand and produce it?"

"There's an Italian restaurant down the road. They gave me one of their menus. All I have to do is ring up an order, and they'll deliver."

"Ah! We don't have to dress."

"I like things to be easy," he declared, clamping her body to his, then hoisting her out of the bath with him in a great whoosh of water. He grabbed a soft, fluffy bath towel and enveloped her in it, his eyes shining their delight in her, and Joanna knew in that moment, with devastating clarity, that her heart had always been his, and probably always would be.

If only he hadn't abused it... But she didn't want to think about that. Not now. Three years *had* passed. Maybe Rory deeply regretted what he had done and would never do it again. What they had together was worth another chance, wasn't it?

"There's a blow-drier above the vanity if you want it," he said when he finished rubbing the wetness from her hair.

"Thanks. I do," she replied lightly, preferring not to leave her long tresses in damp rats' tails.

The bathroom was so large it undoubtedly had every luxurious facility built into it, Joanna thought, her gaze running admiringly over the long vanity bench with its twin wash bowls and gold taps. Rory walked over to a mirrored cupboard, opened it, withdrew two white bathrobes and handed her one of them. Hers was significantly smaller than his, Joanna noted, as they put them on.

"I'll go and get the menu from the kitchen. Read it out to you while you fix your hair," Rory offered with a smile.

"Fine!" she approved, flashing a quick smile at him to hide the sudden lump of lead in her heart. The woman-size bathrobe was not new. It hadn't been waiting for her. It had been used by some other woman, laundered, stored to accommodate whoever else came along to share Rory's bed and bath.

So what did you expect? Joanna savagely berated herself as Rory left her. It was beyond the bounds of reason to imagine Rory Grayson being celibate for three years. Apart from which, she had been in another man's bed. And bathroom.

Logic, however, did not ease the pain she felt at the thought of Rory having some other woman here. It was *her* home, the one she had dreamed of with him. It wasn't fair to bring other women into it and make love to them. Somehow it was almost as bad an infidelity as had driven her out of their marriage.

Joanna gave herself a mental shake. She was being ridiculous. She had divorced Rory, had told him to get out of her life and stay out. He had stated unequivocally he had accepted her word on that, so perhaps what he'd done here was a kind of exorcism, achieving what she had thought impossible, then bringing some other woman into it to prove she no longer mattered to him. In any event, Joanna knew she had no right to judge him on anything he'd done while they were apart.

Nevertheless, it gave her pause to reassess the situation as she moved over to the vanity and began the mechanical task of blow-drying her hair. One perfect afternoon of love and laughter was no basis for making lifetime decisions. The only certainty was that Rory still desired her. There was no promise of anything else in a dirty weekend. She had to keep her head on straight, no matter what her heart told her.

Easier said than done, she thought, when Rory came back and made a happy game of discussing the merits of every item on the restaurant menu with her. His zany good humour was infectious. Joanna could feel her defences melting again and simply gave up on trying to re-erect them.

The next couple of hours were the happiest Joanna had spent in a long time. While they waited for their dinner to be delivered, they relaxed in the living room, nibbling nuts and olives, drinking a delicious white wine, recalling some of the best times they had shared together. Rory played Neil Diamond's "Hot August Night" CD and enticed her into dancing with him. They ended up raucously singing the words they had learnt so many years ago, and collapsing into laughter as they finished the last number.

When their dinner arrived, they were both ravenous. They ate through each course with barely a pause, their appetites heightened by the sheer enjoyment of being in each other's company. Or so it seemed to Joanna.

Somewhere in the back of her mind a cautious voice insisted on reminding her this was only a pretend game, and sooner or later she and Rory would have to face the issues that had split them apart. It wasn't possible to start over again with a clean slate.

Or was it?

Was it really necessary to bring up the bad times? So many of them had been caused by the lack of money, and that was clearly not a problem anymore. Why spoil something so positive with negatives that were no longer relevant?

Joanna lulled herself into contentment with the sense of beautiful harmony between them. Rory clearly had no wish to break it, either. His eyes caressed her with heart-tingling pleasure. There was not the slightest shadow from the past in his manner towards her. It was as though they were rediscovering all that had attracted them to each other in the first place.

Their meal over, Rory put on the more romantic music of Ravel's "Bolero." He insisted Joanna relax on the couch and enjoy listening while he went to the kitchen to make coffee. It was his pleasure to serve her tonight.

Perfection, Joanna thought blissfully, stretching out languorously on the leather cushions. Impulsively she made the decision to sweep the past out of the way once and for all. She was now disposed to concede that perhaps she had been too black and white about Rory's adultery. People did make mistakes. At the time there had been a lot of tensions between them, their marriage far from perfect.

Not enough money to get the job done as well as Rory wanted, not enough money to start the family Joanna yearned for, always having to put off things until Rory achieved the success he was sure would come. Joanna had been fed up with putting off things, especially having a baby. Other couples in poorer circumstances managed to have babies.

Then there was the call from Jessica that their mother was to have a serious heart operation. Could Joanna find it in her heart to effect a reconciliation? If their mother were to die...

Rory hadn't liked the idea of Joanna visiting her mother in hospital without him. Either together or not at all, he had vehemently argued, well aware of Fay Harding's hostility towards him and their marriage. It was a reasonable stance, Joanna knew, but she had worried about upsetting her mother when she was in such a serious condition. She had insisted on going alone.

And on one of those visits to her mother...

Rory came back with the coffee. His eyes glittered over the cleavage revealed by the drooping edges of her bathrobe. His appreciative grin set her pulse racing again. Joanna could not help revelling in Rory's unabated desire for her. She wanted it to go on forever. As she watched him pour coffee, she felt the urgent importance of putting the past behind them.

"Rory..."

"Yes?" He glanced warmly at her.

"I forgive you about Bernice," she said quickly, wanting it over and done with. "I know things weren't good between us at the time, and a lot of it was my fault.''

She saw his face tighten. He hooded his eyes as he set the percolator down on the tray he had placed on the coffee table. To Joanna's consternation, as he straightened up it was all too obvious he didn't take kindly to her well-meant initiative. He wore an air of grimly held control.

''I appreciate your—'' he paused, his mouth curling contemptuously ''—generosity in forgiving me about Bernice, Joanna. I'm sure you feel it's big of you.'' There was a fierce blaze of pride in his eyes as he added, ''But I don't want your forgiveness for something I didn't do.''

Joanna could hardly believe he was denying it again. What point was there in sticking to a lie when she had virtually told him it was no longer an issue between them? Why couldn't he just admit it and let it go, as she was trying to do? She stared at him in hurt bewilderment.

The doorbell rang, adding its discordant sound to the tension between them. The Italian waiter to collect the dishes, Joanna thought, grateful for the interruption that allowed her time to reconsider the position while Rory went to let the man in.

Could Rory have been telling the truth all along? But what of the evidence lined up against him? Why would Bernice make such a serious charge if Rory was innocent of any wrongdoing? Bernice had definitely been pregnant. There was no denying that.

Joanna's feverish train of thought was abruptly shattered by the sound of an angry voice.

Brad's voice!

What was he doing here?

"You've abducted my fiancée! The police have been informed. Stand aside or face the consequences and the full penalties of the law."

Rory gave a droll laugh as he stepped aside to let Brad through. "Joanna," he called out. "I think one of your friends has arrived to rescue you."

She barely had time to absorb the shock before Brad charged into the living room, leaving Rory to follow in his wake. Brad glowered a fierce determination that brooked no opposition. Joanna was forcibly reminded of a bull all steamed up to snort and paw over its territory. It took her a moment to recover wits enough to pull the bathrobe more tightly around her as she scrambled to her feet.

"Brad, what are you doing here?" she cried, appalled by the scene in which she suddenly found herself. "Why aren't you in Brisbane? How did—"

"Your mother called me when she found out you'd been carried off by your ex-husband," he explained before her state of dishabille hit him front on.

Joanna saw his eyes dilate. His face seem to puff out, his skin blotching with angry patches of red. His mouth tightened into a grim slash. His chest rose and fell in quick succession. She tried to think of something to say, but any words of appeasement totally escaped her.

"What has he done to you?" Brad finally spluttered. "What have you been doing together?"

Her dirty weekend with Rory had come home to roost with a vengeance!

CHAPTER SIX

JOANNA'S MIND whirled. She hadn't set out to hurt Brad. All she had meant to do was settle the question of whether or not it was right for her to marry him. Despite those very reasonable intentions, she couldn't see Brad accepting them as any kind of justification for the present circumstances.

She stared back at him, totally tongue-tied, knowing her silence condemned her in his eyes, yet unable to find any words that wouldn't condemn her further.

"I think, Joanna," Rory drawled, "that what you are now seeing is called, in the very best circles, justifiable rage."

"You keep out of it!" Brad snapped. "Or I'll... I'll—" He looked Rory up and down, thought better of making physical threats, then turned furious eyes back to Joanna.

I'm going to be killed, Joanna thought wildly, and for one mad moment wondered if Rory had engineered all this to ruin any possibility of her having a life with Brad.

"Why don't we all sit down and talk seriously and earnestly together as friends over a glass of champagne?" Rory suggested provocatively.

Brad shot Rory a glare that would have shrivelled any schoolboy under his authority. Its only effect was to evoke a waggish grin from his protagonist, so he turned his rage to Joanna. "I demand to know what's going on!"

"I'm sorry, Brad," she started, desperately hunting for the least hurtful words to explain. "I'm terribly sorry you've been put to so much trouble. I needed to see Rory and..."

"Might I point out you do not own Joanna," Rory slid in, his tone dripping with sweet reason. "And you never will. Not even if you marry her. Besides which, until your ring is on her finger, all's fair in love and war."

"Not in my book," Brad retorted, eyeing Rory with blistering contempt. "I have it on good authority you're nothing but a faithless bastard."

"Quoting the infallible and self-righteous Fay Harding, of course," Rory mocked.

Joanna burned with mortification. For her mother to have interfered to this extent was humiliating in the extreme. Getting Brad to leave his conference in Brisbane to fly to Sydney, supposedly on a rescue mission, was more than concern for Joanna's relationship with Brad. It was virtually a declaration of war on Rory Grayson.

"I brought champagne," a female voice trilled from the doorway into the apartment, distracting all three of them from the issue in dispute.

"Ah, Monique!" Rory warbled in warm welcome. "What perfect timing you have! Please come in, my dear."

Joanna was not grateful for the distraction. It was a distraction that raised a lot more questions that needed to be answered. The gorgeous brunette, now in a slinky violet jumpsuit that left no curve unhugged, took the spotlight as she made her entrance on the scene.

Joanna's burning mortification deepened to burning suspicion over what part the beautiful Monique played in Rory's life, arriving on his doorstep with a bottle of champagne at this time of night!

"Who is this?" Brad demanded.

Well might he ask, Joanna thought, turning stormy eyes to Rory for his explanation. What did he think he was doing, inviting in another woman when he had been making love to her all afternoon? Was he seizing the opportunity to flaunt his relationship with Monique as a way of balancing the scales, having been brought face to face with Joanna's relationship with Brad?

The immediate memory of Rory's bitter pride as he rejected her forgiveness over his affair with Bernice rose up to haunt Joanna. What did it mean?

"I suppose you could call Monique my very good friend," he said, a look of saintliness and beatitude spreading over his face.

"Get dressed, Joanna!" Brad commanded. "What we have to say together is best said in private."

Not before I let this woman know that Rory and I have come together again, Joanna swiftly decided. "My clothes are in the master bedroom," she said, giving Monique a meaningful look that she couldn't misinterpret.

It didn't seem to upset the brunette at all. In fact, she eyed Joanna with heightened interest. "Of course they're in the bedroom. Where else would they be?" she said as though it was perfectly reasonable to her.

Which left Joanna flummoxed.

Brad, however, reacted with appropriate explosiveness. "And what, might I ask, are your clothes doing in his bedroom?" he roared.

Oddly enough, Brad's fury floated over Joanna's head. She felt completely detached from it. The realisation came to her that Brad had never been an answer to her needs. Not her deep needs. And she should have known that all along. It was Rory she needed, yet he seemed to be demonstrating he did not need her. Was it pride? Or rejection? Impossible to find out until she got Brad out of her life.

"If you'll all excuse me," she said with as much dignity as she could muster, "I'll go and get changed. Then I'll be leaving."

No-one tried to stop her. As she left the three of them behind in the living room, she heard Monique say brightly, "I have some good news. We found Kawowski."

Joanna's feet almost faltered to a halt. Her mind spun with confusion. How on earth could Kawowski be found when he didn't exist? The hallway to the bedroom stretched in front of her. She pushed her feet forward, but they were slowed by the further bubbly communication from Monique.

"He doesn't make safety matches as you first thought, Rory. He runs a dating service."

Joanna shook her head. It was pure fabrication on her part, wasn't it? Yet if Kawowski was real... Joanna groaned as she remembered the connection, Poppy Dalton telling her about the dating service she was going to try. She hadn't invented it at all. The whole thing had simply slid out of her subconscious.

"He's denying he ever contacted us," Monique said with a ring of scepticism. "Claims he has no use for market research."

"At last! An adversary worthy of my mettle," Rory crowed with relish. "He won't get away with that ploy. I'll nail him down to a contract no matter what it costs. The idea of bringing people together and matching them up appeals to me."

Joanna felt quite dizzy by the time she reached the bedroom door. Everything was such a muddle. Brad, Rory, Monique, Kawowski... One shock after another, and not knowing what Rory's intentions were concerning their relationship.

There seemed little point in confessing what had really happened about Kawowski. Trying to explain why she had used the name to get to Rory would only stir more mud into an already murky area with Brad. Let Rory handle it, she thought defeatedly. He was handling everything else with consummate ease.

Joanna entered the master bedroom and closed out the mess behind her. As her eyes took in the wildly rumpled bed and the clothes strewn around the floor, her heart lurched with the memory of her abandonment with Rory this afternoon. Maybe all he had ever meant to do was get her to stay with him for a dirty weekend. It was she who had tried to make it more, clearing up the misunderstanding about her mother, forgiving him Bernice.

He hadn't accepted either one of her efforts at reconciliation with open arms, reserving judgement about her mother and proudly refusing to admit his guilt over Bernice. Couldn't *he* bring himself to admit to any fault?

Joanna picked up Rory's clothes and dumped them on his bed. With a shudder of revulsion she threw off the bathrobe that Monique had probably worn before her. She started dragging on her clothes, consoling herself with the thought that at least she had sorted herself out about Brad, if nothing else.

She deeply regretted having wasted nine months of Brad's life when he could have spent the time more fruitfully with some other woman, but she truly hadn't known better until today. The fact that he had disrupted his conference for her sake, only to be faced with this awful mire of indignity, made Joanna writhe with guilt and shame. Brad had deserved better from her.

There was a loud rap on the door, then Brad's voice calling out, "Are you ready yet, Joanna?"

The impatient bite in his tone made Joanna close her eyes and take a deep, deep breath. She dreaded this final confrontation, but there was no evading it. She slipped on her shoes, made sure her skirt was straight, then replied, "I'll be with you in a moment," hoping he would retreat to wait for her.

No such luck! The door opened and Brad barged into the bedroom, intent on discovering all there was to discover about the situation that had wreaked havoc with his hopes for the future. Rory and Monique trailed in after him, apparently determined on being in on the action.

"That bed has definitely been slept in," Brad declared accusingly.

"Funny thing that," Rory drawled cheerfully. "It happens every night."

"And he never makes it in the morning," Monique added helpfully. "I know."

Joanna seethed over how frequently Monique had been here to know, and seethed even more over Rory's blithe unconcern in letting her parade the fact. On the other hand, Rory could be inwardly seething over the fact that Brad was here, parading his relationship with Joanna. His arrival on the scene could not have come at a worse time for Joanna.

Brad ignored both Monique and Rory. He glared towering contempt at Joanna. "That puts the seal on it. You can't explain this away. I'd never be able to trust you again, Joanna. You're as guilty as—"

"Now hang on a moment," Rory broke in, his eyebrows slanting down in exaggerated concern. "What do you think happened between Joanna and me?"

"That's perfectly obvious," Brad snapped.

"It certainly isn't obvious to me," Rory retorted with another beatific show of innocence.

"You've been having sexual relations with your ex-wife," Brad fired at him.

Rory stiffened, his mobile face taking on an expression of extreme indignation. "How dare you impugn Joanna's character like that?" he bellowed. "Don't you know she hates me?"

Brad looked somewhat poleaxed by this unexpected counterattack. Joanna felt stunned herself. What game was Rory playing now? She watched in total bewilderment as he advanced on Brad menacingly.

"Do you think she jumps into bed with every man she hates? Is that what you're saying?"

Brad shook his head dazedly. "I was saying—"

"I think you'd better shut up and listen!" Rory advised him, each word loaded with threat. His vivid blue eyes flashed with volatile emotion and his hands flew out in wild gesticulations as he raved on. "If Joanna likes you well enough to go to bed with you, you should get down on your knees and bless your lucky stars, you ingrate! How dare you accuse her of hopping into bed with me! Joanna may have her faults, but I'll tell you this from long years of experience. She is fastidious and discriminating. You'd better learn how to say you're sorry, and you'd better learn it fast."

Rory's heated defence of her good name left Joanna drowning in a sea of confusion. Why had he suddenly decided to protect her from Brad's wrath? Of all the unpredictable things Rory had ever done, this took first prize! What profit was there for him in giving her a chance to make peace with a man he didn't want her to marry?

Or didn't he care about that anymore?

Having had what he wanted from her, was he simply tossing her back into Brad's lap?

She looked at her erstwhile fiancé to see how he had taken the cleverly worded diatribe. Brad's face was breaking out in red splotches again. He was not the kind of man who liked to be found in the wrong.

"If you weren't doing that," he countered, "then what was going on? Why was she undressed?"

"Well," said Rory. "Isn't it perfectly obvious?"

"No, it's not."

Joanna looked at Rory, intrigued as to how he was going to slide out of that corner. Or had his inventiveness run out? He assumed a lofty expression as though he was the headmaster and Brad a recalcitrant pupil.

"That's because you've got a wicked, disgusting, dirty mind," he declared. "It's quite simple, really. I rang Joanna at home and told her I wanted to see her on a matter of—"

"You rang Joanna!" Brad interjected, frowning with suspicion. "Her mother said Joanna rang you."

Rory sighed with pained patience. "I was trying to shortcut the story. I rang Joanna first, but she wouldn't have a bar of me. Then her compassionate nature got the better of her and she rang me back."

"Why did you want to see her?" Brad demanded tersely.

"Because there was unfinished financial business from the time when Joanna supported me. Which I wished to finalise. Joanna acceded to my request on the proviso that we meet at my office so she could feel secure. She refused to take anything from me. I carried her off so I had enough time to make her see sense. There you have it."

"I don't believe this," Brad muttered broodingly. He shot a hard, doubting look at Joanna, but Rory started rattling on again, preventing him from directing any questions at her.

"That's because you spend your time dealing with schoolchildren with their sneaky little minds. In the world of business we're much more straightforward. Now that Joanna has agreed to accept a couple of million dollars—"

"I didn't agree to that!" Joanna cried. He was going too far.

"I told you I wouldn't give you anything to eat until you agreed. You ate all your dinner. Why did you do that if you weren't agreeable?" Rory asked, ringing her in to do whatever she wanted to do with his ever-growing lie. The blue eyes twinkled their devilish challenge, and Joanna wished she hadn't opened her mouth.

"Because I was hungry," she tossed back at him.

Rory cocked his head consideringly. "Reasonable," he said, then turned to Brad. "Anyway, our clothes got wet running through the rain. Joanna had to put hers in the clothes dryer so here we are in bathrobes. Satisfied?"

Brad shook his head. "This is like a nightmare."

"Well, it may not have rained in Brisbane but anyone in Sydney will tell you we had one hell of a storm," Rory burbled on. "Torrential rain. Even Joanna's mother will have to admit that. If she ever gets off her broomstick."

"Yes," said Monique, the trusty ally. "I saw them both running through the rain. It was such a downpour. Drenched to the skin, they were."

Joanna was immediately tempted to blow open the whole stack of lies. It was perfectly obvious what motive Monique had for joining in. She wanted Joanna to get back together with Brad so she wouldn't have to share Rory with his ex-wife.

A strain of hard commonsense held her tongue. This mad explanation was easier to live with than the truth. Especially where Brad was concerned. His ego was going to take enough battering, without the added wound of Joanna's fall from grace with her ex-husband.

There was a thunderous knock from the direction of the door to the apartment. "Police! We're making an entry!" came the loud announcement.

Rory rolled his eyes to the heavens, swung on his heel and went to confront the law. Monique was right behind him like the good and faithful terrier she was. Brad waited, eyeing Joanna warily. She strode out of the bedroom ahead of him with an air of proud disdain. Brad followed.

Two burly policemen stood at the entrance to the living room, eyeing the place with interest. They turned to size up the party coming down the hallway. "Any trouble here?" one asked.

"Ah, officer," Rory rolled out with every evidence of relief and gratitude. "I'm so glad to see you." He pointed at Brad. "This man burst into my home and has been threatening me with aggravated bodily assault. If you could see him off the premises—"

"Now, hold on a moment," the policeman commanded. "That wasn't the complaint we received."

Brad bustled forward, taking Joanna's arm to sweep her with him. "It was about my fiancée, whom I've now recovered." He pointed at Rory. "That man abducted her."

The policeman directed his attention to Joanna. "Are you Miss Joanna Harding?"

"Yes, Officer, but there's been a terrible misunderstanding," she put in quickly. "Mr. Grayson here—" she nodded at Rory "—was trying to give me a couple of million dollars and—" She clamped her mouth shut, appalled that she had been caught up in this outlandish fiction of Rory's. But what else could she do?

The officer heaved a lugubrious sigh. "Lady, I've had a very hard day. I really have. This call came through as we were going off duty. Are you, or are you not, being held here against your will?"

"No, I'm not. In fact, I'm leaving right now with this man from Brisbane," she said firmly. Her sense of humanity insisted that she let Brad down in private and as soon as possible. Especially when he had put himself out so far for her sake.

"You poor thing," Monique sympathised, stepping forward to touch the officer's arm and dazzling him with her smile. "Fancy being loaded with a false alarm when you look as though you're worked to death. Do come and sit down. Both of you. And I'll pour you a glass of champagne."

They were instantly charmed out of their weariness. "I'd rather have a beer," the older policeman said.

"Me, too," the other chimed in, grinning at Monique as though she was a gift from the gods.

"Of course. I'll get you both a beer."

"Let's go, Joanna," Brad grated in frustration with the situation.

"It will be my pleasure to see you out," Rory said with a gracious wave towards the door. "And please feel free to call me for anything at all, Joanna. You know I have your future happiness at heart."

Joanna stared miserably at the sparkling challenge in his eyes, then swept past him, hating the way Monique had taken over as hostess as though well accustomed to it, and hating having to go with Brad when she desperately wanted to straighten everything out with Rory.

"I'll put the cheque for two million in the mail for you, Joanna," he called after her as she and Brad headed for the elevator.

And I'll tear it up if you do, she silently vowed, refusing to acknowledge Rory's wickedly teasing curtain line.

"This has been the worst day of my life," Brad muttered.

"I am sorry about that, Brad," she said on a bleak sigh of resignation, knowing the worst was yet to come for him.

The elevator doors opened. Joanna stepped inside the compartment that would take her away from Rory. Would he call her? Or did he mean she would have to call him if there was to be any future happiness for them? He had said he would never chase after her again.

When she turned around she found he was propped in the doorway to his apartment, watching her, a crooked little smile tilting his mouth. Then as the elevator doors began to close he blew her a kiss, irreverent, totally careless of what Brad might think, provocative to the very end.

Was it a kiss goodbye? Or was it a promise he would be here for her if she did call?

Probably the most important question was when would he get rid of Monique? He had given her short shrift in the office today. Would he give her short shrift tonight?

CHAPTER SEVEN

BRAD LED JOANNA to a hired car he'd picked up at the airport. More expense to the costly exercise of flying to her rescue, she thought grimly. Her mother had a lot to answer for.

With his punctilious courtesy, Brad saw her settled in the passenger seat. Joanna stiffly thanked him. Brad said nothing until he was safely esconced behind the wheel. His first words were as strained as the silence had been between them.

"I'm sorry, Joanna. It seems that I leapt to unwarranted conclusions. Your mother led me to believe that your ex-husband was capable of anything."

"My mother has always had an extreme prejudice against Rory," Joanna stated flatly. "I'm sorry she dragged you into this, Brad."

"I considered it was in our best interests. I can't afford a scandal, Joanna. And having now met your ex-husband, I understand your mother's concern. He's certainly a reprehensible character. No moral fibre at all."

Joanna bit her tongue, cutting off the impulse to defend Rory's character. Brad would never understand it, anyway. He was as conventional as her mother. Why hadn't she realised what a narrow rut she had been digging for herself all this time? A reaction against Rory, she surmised, but it had been blindly stupid to get as deeply involved with Brad as she had.

"I must say I find it very surprising that he's willing to compensate you for all you did for him when you were married," Brad went on. "Which, of course, he should."

Joanna gritted her teeth at this last comment. She shot Brad a dark look. Did he think money made everything better? "I'd like to go home, Brad," she said, impatient with his moralising.

"Yes," he agreed, switching on the engine. "It's best we relieve your mother's anxiety as soon as possible."

That was another scene Joanna was not looking forward to, but her most immediate concern was to make it clear to Brad she was not his fiancée, which he had been claiming all night, and was never going to be his fiancée. By her figuring, the distance across the city from Dee Why to Burwood gave her about an hour to state her position and convince Brad she meant it.

However, they were no sooner on their way than Brad picked up on the money angle again. "We could do a lot with two million dollars, Joanna."

A black cynicism blotted out her mental attempts at finding a tactful rejection of his marriage proposal. No doubt it was now in Brad's best interests to forget all his suspicions about what had happened in Rory's apartment. Such a bonanza to a bank account, hopefully a *joint* bank account, clearly made moral fibre a lot less important.

"I do not intend to accept one cent from Rory," she said coldly.

Brad frowned. "But if he owes it to you—"

"He doesn't. Not in my book."

"He said you supported him," Brad argued.

"I was his wife. As far as I'm concerned, supporting my husband was part of my commitment to our marriage."

Brad chewed over this high moral ground for several moments before coming up with a sidestep. "I think it would be a kindness to free him of guilt, Joanna."

She thought about Bernice and wondered if Rory had spoken the truth. If so, she had left him for nothing, and all the pain had been for nothing. "I don't think Rory feels any guilt," she said slowly. "Pride, yes. Guilt, no."

Brad shook his head in paternal reproof. "It's time you gave up this hatred of your ex-husband. After all, if you're marrying me—"

"I'm not." Irritated by Brad's pontificating, the words slipped off her tongue before Joanna could catch them back and couch them in more acceptable terms.

Brad glanced sharply at her. "Not what? Giving up your hatred?"

She closed her eyes, inhaled a deep breath, then quietly but firmly closed the gate on Brad's hopes and expectations. "I'm not marrying you, Brad. I'm not sure I'm fit to marry anyone."

"That's ridiculous, Joanna. I realise you're upset about—"

"I'm not upset. I've simply come to a decision. I'm sorry for having wasted your time, Brad, but seeing Rory today made up my mind for me. I need to sort out a lot of things before I think of marrying again. If I ever do."

Brad used every argument he could think of on the way to her mother's home. None of them impressed Joanna. In fact, the more Brad said, the more she realised he didn't love her. She was his main chance for what he saw as a suitable marriage partner. That was all. And she would have been an even better main chance with Rory's millions.

As the car came to a halt outside her Burwood address, she turned to him and drew a line of finality through their relationship. "I think it best if you release me from my teaching contract with the school, Brad. Effective immediately. Neither of us will feel comfortable if I continue there. I'm sure you appreciate that."

"You won't find it easy getting another position at short notice," he warned her, still fighting to change her mind.

"That's my problem. Thank you for bringing me home." Joanna turned to him and made one last attempt to soften the blow of her rejection, taking all the blame upon herself. "I'm sorry for any hurt I've done you, but a marriage between us wouldn't work for me, Brad, and because of that, it couldn't work for you. You'll be much happier with some other woman who isn't damaged by a previous marriage."

"Joanna..." His eyes met hers in pained appeal, reminding her there had been much between them she had enjoyed, much they had shared with pleasure. "Please reconsider. Is this the impulse of the moment, or a sound decision?"

"It's the latter, Brad," she said softly.

His face tightened in bitter defeat. "You're going back to Rory Grayson? Is that what's happening?"

"I don't know." She shook her head as a wave of sadness washed through her. If she had done Rory the injury of not believing him when he was innocent of adultery, did he really want her back? "Right at this moment, I feel more alone than I've ever felt before."

"You don't have to be."

"I'm sorry, Brad." She looked at him with implacable resolve. Nothing good could come from shilly-shallying. "Believe me. I am sorry. But it's better for you if we make a clean break now."

"So be it, then," he said in weary resignation.

"Thank you." She reached across and gently pressed his hand. "Goodbye, Brad."

He stared grimly ahead, not acknowledging the last farewell, probably seeing all his bright plans crumbling into dust. Stabbed by guilt at her part in clouding his future, Joanna cut the agony short by opening her own door and stepping out without another word. Brad had made a mistake with her. She had made a mistake with him. She closed the door on both mistakes and turned away.

Two things happened simultaneously. Brad drove off. The front door of the house opened. Clearly her mother had been keeping watch for someone to come, either Joanna or Brad or both of them.

Joanna walked slowly up the front path, knowing that the three-year truce with her mother had come to an end. Tonight was turning out to be a watershed in her life. The end of Brad, the end of her teaching job at Brad's school, the start of a life of complete independence.

"Who was that who brought you home, Joanna?" her mother asked sharply.

"The knight in shining armour that you summoned from Brisbane," she replied with caustic humour.

"Oh, dear! I was afraid of that." Pure anguish dripped from her voice. "I suppose he caught you with Rory Grayson."

Joanna paused, face to face with her mother at the doorway. Her grey eyes were as cold as winter as she replied, "No. He didn't. But Brad did charge into Rory's home with all the suspicions you put into his mind. I hope you're satisfied with your meddling, Mum." Then she stepped past her into the front hall and headed straight for the telephone.

The door closed behind her with more force than it was used to. "I got in touch with Brad before you called home, Joanna," her mother cried. Her voice gathered strength with self-justification. "What was I supposed to do? Leave you in the clutches of Rory Grayson?"

"I'm not a child, Mum." Joanna wheeled on her to set the record straight. "And let me tell you I'm a lot safer in Rory's clutches than I am in yours."

Her mother stiffened in affront. "How can you possibly say that? He's a—"

"He cared more about my good name than you did," Joanna cut in bitterly. "You placed me in the most invidious, humiliating position that any mother could put a daughter in. And it was Rory who rescued me from it. Rory who put all Brad's suspicions to rest. And you know why he did that, Mum?"

It was a rhetorical question. Joanna didn't wait for a reply. "He did it so that I was left with a free choice as to what I wanted to do with my life. He cleared away the trouble you had created. He gave me the chance to carry on with my relationship with Brad as though nothing at all had happened to disrupt it. He wiped the slate clean of the dirt you'd piled onto it. That's what he did. So don't you dare turn up your nose at Rory Grayson. Ever again!"

While her mother was still suffering shell shock, Joanna swung to the telephone table, picked up the receiver, dialled the taxi service she usually patronised and ordered a car for fifteen minutes.

It snapped her mother into battle mode. "You're not going back to him!" she protested vehemently.

"No. Not tonight. Though I may in the future. I've just severed all connection with Brad." Her eyes slashed hard decision at her mother. "And I don't want to be with you right now or I'll end up saying things I might later regret."

She dialled Poppy Dalton's number, and her friend and fellow teacher answered on the second ring. "Hi! It's Joanna. I know it's late, but do you mind if I come over and stay the night?"

"I'd love you to," Poppy enthused. "I'm feeling miserable and lonely."

"That makes two of us. I'll be there in about half an hour, Poppy."

It only took her ten minutes to sweep all she wanted into a suitcase. Her mother had followed her to the bedroom and watched the furious activity with growing alarm.

"You don't need all that for an overnight stay, Joanna," she observed.

"I don't know how long it will take me to find a place of my own, but when I do, I'll come back for the rest of my things."

"Joanna, please . . . We have to talk."

"You went too far, Mum."

"I didn't mean to hurt you and Brad," she cried in very real anguish. "I tried to call him back after I heard from you, but he'd already left the hotel in Brisbane. Can't you patch it up with him, Joanna?"

"I don't want to." Her eyes flashed bitter resentment. "You never did listen to what I want, did you, Mum? It always had to be your judgement that was right."

"I only ever wanted what was best for you, Joanna."

"What *you* considered best. And please don't say any more, Mum. I don't want to hate you more than I do at the present moment."

Her mother's face paled. She sat down shakily on the side of the bed. Joanna hesitated a moment, worried about her mother's heart. The doctors had said the new valve was working perfectly. There was no cause for concern. Besides, her mother needed to be shocked into evaluating their relationship. Joanna firmly dismissed the niggle of concern and went to the bathroom to collect her toiletries.

When she returned to the bedroom her mother was still sitting where she had left her. Her face was a better colour. Recovery rate rapid, Joanna thought with dry irony. She made room for her toiletries in the suitcase, then zipped the bag shut.

"I'm sorry, Joanna," her mother offered with a pained look.

"Are you, Mum?" Joanna challenged, her heart hardening with the memory of all the problems her mother had caused. "Were you ever sorry that you didn't give me a wedding to remember, like Jessica's? Were you sorry that you turned your back on me for marrying the man I loved? That you hurt and never helped? Were you sorry when I came home with my heart bleeding?"

"He wasn't right for you," came the truculent and predictable defence.

"I loved him. I'll never love another man as I loved Rory Grayson. I'll probably never know again the happiness I once had with him. I'm sorry you don't understand that, Mum. I'm sorry you never cared enough about my feelings to try to understand."

"That's not true!" her mother protested. "It was his influence that came between us."

Joanna shook her head. "It had to be your way or there was no way at all. Well, now I'm going my way. For good. And if you want to have any part of my life, you'd better start accepting that."

"This is harming my health. It could kill me," her mother said in a quavering voice. "How can you leave me like this?"

"Ring Jessica!"

Joanna picked up her suitcase, marched out of the bedroom and straight out of the house. Tears blurred her eyes, and she could hardly see a step in front of her. Stupid to break down now, she berated herself. It was not that she lacked strength of purpose. It was simply that she felt terribly alone, stripped bare of all that had sustained her during the years apart from Rory. And she didn't know if he really wanted her in his life again. Desire was one thing, trust and commitment quite another. Could one ever repair what had been deeply damaged?

She heard a car pull up. The sign glowing on its roof identified it as the taxi. Its timing could not have been better. The driver took her suitcase. Joanna slumped into the back seat for the last journey of the night. At least there would be a sympathetic ear at the end of it, she consoled herself, and grimly worked on regaining her composure before she got to Poppy's.

CHAPTER EIGHT

POPPY DALTON lived in the adjoining suburb of Croydon. Eight years ago, she had come to the conclusion it was highly unlikely any man was going to come along and sweep her off her feet, so she decided to invest in her own future and a small semidetached terrace house.

Originally the house had consisted of two bedrooms, living room, kitchenette, bathroom and a small laundry room. Poppy had turned the second bedroom into a music room cum personal study, but it contained a divan bed for overnight guests. Joanna had often stayed there, and was assured of a warm welcome.

Poppy was wearing an all-enveloping navy blue woollen dressing-gown when Joanna arrived. Like all her clothes, it was solid quality, yet lacking in any attractive femininity. Poppy had given up on her looks almost a decade ago, deciding that red hair was awful, freckled skin worse, and she didn't have *it* where men were concerned anyway.

Her bright hazel eyes lit with questions when she saw Joanna's suitcase. "I'm moving on tomorrow," Joanna explained. "My mother and I have reached the parting of the ways."

"Ah! Domestic blues! I've got just the thing for it," Poppy assured her. "You can tell me your woes over the most sinful French pastries you've ever tasted. I bought a pile of them this afternoon."

"Not for me, thanks, Poppy. My stomach's a churning mess. But coffee would be good."

"How about Irish? Sounds like you could do with a shot of whisky."

"You're not wrong," Joanna said ruefully.

"Dump your bag and join me in the living room. A tonic for trouble coming right up."

Despite Poppy's initial show of cheerfulness, she was shocked at the news that Joanna had broken off with Brad. To her, Brad Latham was almost as perfect a man as a woman could get.

Joanna didn't mention anything about Rory. That was too close to her heart to be open for discussion. Yet Poppy, with barely a hint to work on, leapt to the conclusion that Joanna's marriage and divorce had left her with psychological and emotional scars that prevented her from marrying Brad. She had read about such problems and understood they put people off making a permanent commitment to another relationship.

Joanna smothered a wry smile. Poppy had read everything about real-life experiences. It was her substitute for living real-life experiences herself. She was shy, inhibited and lacked confidence in herself, except when she was teaching music. She was a gifted teacher, capable of holding a class of pupils enthralled with her own enthusiasm and love for her subject, yet in any social situation she had a tendency to sink into the nearest wall, unheard and unnoticed.

If Joanna hadn't worked at drawing her out, they would have remained staff acquaintances. It was the occasional flash of dry, secretive humour in Poppy's eyes that had intrigued Joanna into getting to know her better. Although they were opposites in many ways, it was that sense of humour that allowed an easy friendship.

"I'm going to miss having you to talk to at school," Poppy remarked regretfully. "But I guess you're right about its being too embarrassing to stay." Her eyes expressed concern as she added, "What are you going to do about a job?"

Joanna shrugged. "Put my name down on the list at the education department. Watch for ads from private schools. And in the meantime, see if I can get some casual teaching work."

Poppy frowned. "It's not going to be easy, Joanna. Everyone's hanging onto their positions because of the recession."

"I'll find something."

Maybe a change of career would do her good as well, Joanna thought, deciding to peruse all the positions vacant in the newspaper tomorrow. Why should she limit herself to teaching? She was free to do anything she fancied, with no obligations or responsibilities to anyone but herself.

"Well, until you're settled in a job somewhere, why don't you stay here with me?" Poppy suggested brightly. "If you're really determined to live away from your mother, you don't want to tie yourself up with a lease on a place that might be unsuitable. What if you end up working on the other side of the city?''

It was a valid point, but Joanna was reluctant to impose on her friend. Poppy's small house was very much her personal home, furnished with a plethora of knick-knacks and articles she had picked up on her travels over the years. It was so cluttered it tended to make Joanna feel claustrophobic, and she was sure she would end up getting in Poppy's way, or disturbing her friend's fussy fastidiousness over how things should be done.

An overnight stay was easily acceptable. An extended and open-ended length of time in close proximity might be a considerable strain on both of them. Apart from which, Joanna wanted to strike out on her own.

Being with Rory again had driven home the truth that she had lost touch with her real self in burying what she had once shared with him. She needed to break out of the self-protective cocoon she had unwittingly spun around herself, and meet the world on terms that she dictated. Free and independent. Only after she had achieved that would she feel ready to approach Rory again. If he didn't make contact with her.

''It's very kind of you, Poppy, but—''

''Oh, please do,'' Poppy pressed, and to Joanna's astonishment, flushed a bright red. ''I would really appreciate your help, Joanna.''

Her friend looked so discomfited, Joanna's sympathy was instantly aroused. ''Of course, I'll help you, Poppy. Tell me what the problem is.''

"Well, I did tell you I was thinking of doing it, and this morning I did it."

"Did what?"

Poppy's eyes were agonised with doubt as she confessed, "I went to Matchmakers Incorporated. That dating service I told you about."

Joanna barely stopped herself from groaning. Was she to be forever haunted by the wretched company she thought she had invented?

"I had to fill out masses of forms and questionnaires and they wanted to make a video of me," Poppy rushed on. "But I put that off because it was too dreadfully embarrassing. As it was, writing down all those things about myself made me feel—" she shuddered "—almost naked."

Hence the French pastries, Joanna concluded. She should have recognised Poppy's state of mind before. Any emotional disturbance brought on a compulsion for rich, gooey food, which then compounded Poppy's weight problem, which then depressed her further and made her more introverted. It was a self-defeating cycle that Joanna had tried to point out to her friend, to no avail.

"I'm not sure I can go through with it," Poppy wailed.

"You don't have to if you don't want to," Joanna soothed.

"But I've already paid over the money and..." She grimaced. "What other chance have I got? I'm thirty-four, Joanna. I've been around the world. I thought I was resigned to living out my life as a spinster, but I look ahead and see myself growing old and more and more lonely. Maybe they can find someone else like me in their files. A nice man who isn't looking for too much..."

"Maybe they can," Joanna agreed, although she was afraid that some *nice* man might take Poppy to the cleaners, fleecing her of her hard-earned worldly goods. How reputable were Mr. Kawowski and Matchmakers Incorporated?

"Anyway, as an introductory thing, Mr. Kawowski is arranging a dinner for six supposedly compatible people, three men and two other women besides myself, for next Saturday night."

"Where's the dinner?" Joanna asked suspiciously.

"It's at the Park Lane Hotel opposite Hyde Park in the city. All perfectly respectable. I can leave and get a taxi right at the door if I don't like the company."

"Sounds reasonable," Joanna acknowledged.

"Oh, yes!" There was tremulous relief in Poppy's voice. "I couldn't have faced a one-on-one situation. Not to begin with."

"So what's the problem?"

"I'm the problem!" Poppy cried in anguish. "I always am. I'll get tongue-tied. I know I will. I need you to coach me, Joanna. And to help me choose a nice outfit. You always look so smart and fashionable. I thought... well, you know how in women's magazines they sometimes make someone over. New hairdo, make-up, clothes. If you would try doing that for me..."

"Are you truly serious about that, Poppy?" Joanna asked.

She nodded, her eyes pleading for support. "I want to look as good as I can. Just once. I know it's asking a lot of you..."

"It'll be my pleasure. I'll stay with you this week to help you all I can, but I'm warning you now, you can't be half-hearted about it. That spinster bun you put your gorgeous hair in has got to go."

"If you say so," she acceded meekly.

"And the French pastries," Joanna declared without mercy. "Tomorrow we shop for slimmers' food. I'm going to put you on a diet and exercise plan that'll trim you down a clothes size before we go shopping. Okay?"

Poppy groaned. "Do I have to?"

"Think of it as a watershed in your life," Joanna said piously.

There might as well be two of them at watersheds, she thought, and doing her best to change Poppy's life around would be an inspiration in changing her own.

"More like white water canoeing," Poppy said grimly. "But you're right. I've got to give it my best shot."

She stood up, squared her shoulders, picked up the plate of French pastries, strode into the kitchenette and dumped them into the garbage bin. She grinned at Joanna. "I promise I won't get up in the middle of the night and fish them out again."

IN SOME WAYS the arrangement they made brought a deepening of their friendship, a trust shared, a sharpening of purpose in their lives. In the days that followed the watershed night, Joanna was glad she had responded to Poppy's appeal. Not only was her friend good company, she also provided the time and space for Joanna to work on her own personal affairs. Making decisions was a first step. Implementing them was going to require some hard thinking and a lot of effort.

On Monday morning a courier arrived, redirected to Poppy's house by Joanna's mother. Joanna signed for the package, which contained a formal letter from Brad, releasing her from her contract with his school.

Since there was no retrieving the situation, he couldn't get rid of me fast enough, Joanna thought. Nevertheless, he had been decent enough to attach a good reference to the letter of release, and that could very well be helpful in acquiring another teaching position. Except teaching seemed to have lost its appeal to her.

The problem was she wasn't qualified for anything else. She had hunted through the newspapers, looking for something to interest her, but most employers were stipulating work experience she simply did not have, and at twenty-nine she was hardly a junior whom they might be willing to train. Was she, in all practical terms, locked into teaching English and history for the rest of her life?

Joanna was brooding over this unattractive prospect when a second courier presented himself on Poppy's doorstep. He delivered another package that required Joanna's signature on a declaration of receipt. Since she had never had dealings with a courier before, two in one day formed quite a milestone in her life.

However, the contents of the second package were far too serious for Joanna to retain any equilibrium at all. She stared at the cheque for two million dollars with sheer disbelief for several seconds. Rory Grayson's signature on it made it real, but she still found it difficult to accept he had gone through with sending it to her.

Attached to the cheque was a brief note. Joanna read it several times, unable to make up her mind what it meant in terms of Rory's feelings about her.

Are you still going to marry Brad? If so, I think I deserve an invitation to the wedding. Don't you?
                    Rory

The cheque had to be to cover her with Brad in case the marriage was still on, Rory protecting her future happiness. But didn't he realise she couldn't marry Brad after what she had shared with him last Friday? Was infidelity irrelevant to Rory? Perhaps he saw no harm in a bit of sex on the side so long as it wasn't found out. Did he think his affair with Bernice had nothing to do with his marriage?

Joanna shook her head. She couldn't accept that kind of thinking. And since Rory had once again proclaimed his innocence over the Bernice affair, Joanna didn't know what to think.

Having gone to preposterous lengths to rescue her relationship with Brad, he certainly deserved an invitation to the hypothetical wedding, but he couldn't want one. Was this his way of finding out what had happened between her and Brad?

The flippant style could be a way of protecting himself from another rejection from her if he was testing her feelings about him. The cheque was definitely Rory at his most provocative, forcing a reply of some kind or other. He knew she didn't want the money. Or did he?

There'd been so many arguments between them about money and how it should be best spent. Priorities that had seemed clear when they had first married had gradually blurred for Joanna as the years went on. Rory had been brought up in foster homes, never having known a real family. What he hadn't had he didn't miss. Having virtually lost her family in marrying him, Joanna had yearned for one of her own, losing patience with Rory's obsession with his theories for which everything else seemed to be sacrificed.

Well, at least she could prove something to him about the money, Joanna thought, and if he did want to know what she had done about Brad, she certainly had no reservations about telling him she was free of any commitment to anyone.

She borrowed some notepaper and an envelope from Poppy and took considerable satisfaction in tearing up the cheque into tiny pieces so Rory received that message loud and clear. She took longer over constructing a short but succinct note in reply to his.

The confetti I made of the unnecessary cheque is in lieu of a wedding invitation. Thank you for showing me I could never marry Brad, and for giving me the chance to part from him with some grace.

Joanna

As she sealed everything in the envelope she wondered if Rory had ended his intimate relationship with Monique.

She considered using a courier for express service, finally discarding the idea in favour of the normal postal service. One day didn't matter in the overall scheme of things, and Rory's note wasn't exactly encouraging in giving her hope for a meaningful reconciliation with him. If it was an approach at all, it was very oblique.

Having posted her reply to Rory, Joanna took Poppy to her hairdresser for the first major step of constructing a new image. She stayed with her the whole time, four hours in all, quelling the panic of having the long, thick tresses cut to shoulder length, then talking her through the trauma of a permanent wave that would put bounce and body into the new hairstyle.

The result was stunning. Poppy did have gorgeous hair. Softly rippling away from her face in a cleverly layered cut of waves and curls, and put through a special conditioning process, the hated red hair took on gleams of gold, and the overall effect cut at least five years off Poppy's age. She was so delighted she couldn't stop looking in mirrors for the rest of the day.

"I'll never be able to keep it like this!" she cried.

"Nonsense! I'll teach you how to use a blow-drier," Joanna promised. "Until you can manage it yourself, a weekly visit to the salon won't break you. And you'll need to get regular trims. At least every six weeks."

They spent the next day at a beauty clinic. A specialist in colour charts instructed Poppy on what colours would suit her and be most flattering when

choosing clothes and make-up. A cosmetician showed
her what could be done to highlight her best features
and minimise flaws. Poppy allowed her eyebrows to be
plucked into a more attractive arch, but she stubbornly baulked at having her ears pierced, insisting she
could buy screw-ons. A manicure completed the revo-
lutionary treatment.

On Wednesday morning, Joanna was putting Poppy
through an aerobics session when the doorbell demanded an interruption. Joanna answered it, only to
be faced with another courier delivering a package to
her. She tore the bag open, expecting some further
missive from Rory, and was astonished to find a pink,
rose-scented envelope, addressed to her in what could
only be a lady's handwriting.

Curiosity aroused, she slit the envelope open and
withdrew the folded pink and rose-scented notepaper.
The message written on it quickly turned curiosity into
a grin of happy relief.

Dear Joanna,
I thought you might tear this letter up if you knew
it was from me so I'm now in disguise to get past
your busy fingers. It took my staff and me nearly
half an hour to count the confetti and no doubt
you will be pleased to know there were 137 pieces.
It takes real conviction to get them down so small.
Well done.

Joanna's initial amusement faded into a serious
weighing as she read on.

If you have nothing momentous to do this Sunday, perhaps you might like to join me for lunch at the Pavilion in the Park. I've booked a table for twelve noon. Good food, a glass of wine, a stroll to idle away the afternoon. No need to let me know. Just come if you want to.

Rory

No chasing after her, Joanna noted, but he was offering her a meeting place, and time enough to consider if she seriously wanted to resume a relationship with him.

At least she now knew that Rory had wanted more than a dirty weekend with her. She didn't know for certain if he had parted with Monique, but Joanna decided she was not going to let the gorgeous brunette deter her from a reconciliation with Rory. After all, Rory had claimed he felt they were right together, even when things were wrong, and he had never felt that with any other woman.

"Joanna?" Poppy called down the hallway. "Is there something wrong?"

"No. Something right." She smiled at her friend. "An offer for an interview. My future's looking brighter."

"That's great!"

"Now let's get back to that aerobics routine."

Poppy was so inspired by her make over that she eagerly kept to the diet and exercise regimen Joanna had stipulated. She practised with the blow-drier, practised applying the new range of cosmetics she had bought and took immense satisfaction in standing on the bathroom scales each morning to measure her weight loss. By Friday she no longer had a roll of fat around her waist and was happily looking forward to their shopping trip.

Armed with her colour chart and trusting enough to take Joanna's advice, she threw conservative caution to the winds and bought boldly. Clothes, shoes, costume jewellery, even some wickedly sexy lingerie was added to the pile of purchases.

"I've never had so much fun in my life!" Poppy declared on their way home. "I'll never be able to thank you enough for all this, Joanna."

"It's been fun for me, too, Poppy," Joanna assured her.

It was certainly some light relief from the serious matter of finding work. There had been no joy at the education department for her in regard to a job. They had a three-year backlist of teachers waiting for any opening that came up. As a result, the list of teachers available for casual work was also formidably long, with little chance of joy there, either. Maybe she should apply for any job at all as a stopgap.

She spent most of Saturday coaching Poppy on social chitchat that would break the ice when meeting strangers. Mr. Kawowski had sent a list of names and résumés of the other five people attending the dinner, and that made preparation easier. Two of the men sounded reasonably promising.

Robert Carr was a widower and managed a bookstore. He listed music amongst his interests. Jack Beaumont was a bachelor and a research chemist by profession. Like Poppy, he had done a lot of travelling, so they should have plenty of memories to share and talk about.

"I wouldn't bother too much with Isaac Stone," Joanna advised, looking over his résumé. "He's divorced. Take it from me. Divorced people are damaged."

"You know so much," Poppy murmured admiringly.

They covered what she could say about herself, how to ask questions of the other people to show interest in them, current affairs that could be brought up for discussion, topics of common interest like her experiences in foreign countries.

By the time Poppy was ready for her dinner date that evening she was primed for anything and everything Joanna could think of. She also looked extremely smart and sophisticated in a bright lime-green blazer, black dress with lime-green piping on the belt, black patent high heels and handbag, a couple of gold chains around her neck and long, dangly gold earrings.

"Feel good about yourself?" Joanna asked with an approving grin.

"Yes, I do," Poppy said in a surprised voice, then grinned with new confidence.

Joanna waved her off, promising to stay up to hear a report when Poppy returned home. She spent most of the intervening hours constructing résumés for herself, having decided to apply for three jobs that sounded within her capabilities, one as a research assistant to a university professor of history, another as sales person for encyclopaedias, the last as an interviewer for a market research company. After all, she had first-hand knowledge of that experience from doing weekend work for Rory years ago.

Her mind drifted to her meeting with Rory tomorrow. Had she wronged him terribly by believing Bernice's claim that he was the father of her baby? Rory had sworn the only relationship he'd ever had with Bernice was that of employer-employee. But that had given him opportunity and temptation, considering the rocky state of their marriage at the time.

Joanna found it difficult to wipe the image of Bernice from her mind, the glazed look of utter disillusionment in the other woman's eyes as Rory had denied ever touching her, let alone been intimate with her, the strange blank set of her face, as though she had expected this betrayal and knew there was no hope of anything good happening for her. More than any words spoken, it was the way Bernice looked that had convinced Joanna she spoke the truth.

If it wasn't the truth, why would Bernice lie, and remain totally steadfast in her lie in the face of Rory's vehement denials? It made no sense to Joanna. She wanted to believe Rory now. She wanted to trust in his love for her. Should she bring the subject up again? Did Rory have some explanation that made sense of it? She resolved to give him the benefit of the doubt and listen to whatever he said with an open mind.

She heard Poppy opening the front door. Joanna's attention was galvanised by the bright cheerfulness of Poppy's voice being answered by a resonant male voice.

Poppy had brought one of the men home with her!

Joanna shot out of her armchair and into the kitchenette, not knowing how else to make herself scarce. She hoped the man was really nice. Would it be Robert Carr or Jack Beaumont? Whoever it was, Joanna wanted it to lead to something positive for her lonely friend.

"There! You'll be comfortable in this chair," she heard Poppy say in fussy consideration. "I won't be a minute putting the coffee on."

She came bouncing into the kitchenette, her face aglow with excitement and pleasure. "Oh, Joanna! I've met the most wonderful man," she whispered.

"Who?" Joanna whispered back. "Jack or Robert?"

"Neither. Isaac Stone. The others were as dull as dishwater compared to him. It doesn't matter that he's divorced. He's not damaged. Except for his eye."

"What's wrong with his eye?"

"I think his wife blinded him. But only in one eye. He wears a black patch. It's really very attractive. He uses a walking stick, too, because he finds it hard to judge distances."

"His wife must have been a Tartar to do that to him."

"Very passionate, he said. But he wasn't interested in talking about her. He was so interested in me, Joanna, he swapped places at the table halfway through the dinner so we could talk more easily. I've had a marvellous time."

"That's great, Poppy! I'm really happy for you. I'll just slip off to bed now and leave you with him."

"I'll introduce you first. Come on."

Poppy linked her arm with Joanna's and proudly marched her into the living room. "Isaac, this is my friend I was telling you about. Joanna Harding."

Joanna stared incredulously at the man who rose to greet her. His tall, athletic body was conservatively dressed in a smart navy blazer, grey trousers, white shirt and red and navy striped tie. He leaned rakishly on his walking stick. The black patch accentuated the vivid blue of his other eye.

"Hello, Joanna," he drawled.

The thump of shock to her heart gave way to a blinding rush of pain, the pain of Rory's perfidy that she had all but put aside a few moments ago. It gave rise to a bitter anger for being fooled into beginning to trust him.

If she hadn't been here, would Poppy have become another Bernice, bowled over by Rory's looks and charm? He'd lied about his name and his supposedly blind eye. How many other lies had he told?

"Rory Grayson," Joanna drawled at him in bitter contempt. "You ought to be stoned to death for this. You're nothing but a low-down deceiving heart-breaker."

CHAPTER NINE

POPPY LOOKED from Rory to Joanna and back to Rory in dazed bewilderment. "You two know each other?"

Joanna glared mockingly at Rory, waiting to hear his admission, challenging him to explain away his heartless deception to a woman who had been completely taken in by his false presentation of himself.

After one derisive flash of his unpatched eye, Rory ignored her. He walked over to Poppy and took her hands, pressing a warm reassurance as he spoke with appealing sincerity. "Whatever happens from here on in, I want you to know I had a good time with you tonight. You had a good time, too, didn't you, Poppy?"

"Yes. Yes, I did," she replied, a definite note of assertion breaking through her confusion.

He lifted her hands and swept a soft kiss over both of them. "Thank you for your delightful company."

This charming piece of gallantry had Poppy bridling with pleasure until better sense forced her to recognise facts. "So what are you?" she asked, searching his face for the truth. "Some kind of criminal or con man?"

Joanna approved that question. Let Rory talk his way out of this and still retain Poppy's belief and admiration!

"When did you meet Joanna?" he asked.

Poppy frowned at the indirectness of his reply. "It was about eighteen months ago. When I joined the staff at the school where she teaches."

"After she was divorced."

"Yes. She'd been married to an absolute scoundrel, and rather than keep his name, she—" Poppy's mouth dropped open in aghast recollection. "Grayson! It was you!" She recoiled from him in horror. "You were the one who did that awful thing to Joanna!"

"Yes. I was that man," he acknowledged with a smile of weary resignation. He removed the black eye patch and shoved it into a blazer pocket as he turned to Joanna. His eyes were a flat, hard blue. "Whatever you personally believe, does it give you joy to blacken my character to others, Joanna?"

Her chin instantly lifted in disdain of the unfair reproof. "You bring it upon yourself, Rory. You're beneath contempt to play with Poppy's feelings when—"

"I know you won't believe me, Joanna," he cut in tersely, "but I wasn't pretending to enjoy Poppy's company. I did. And the reason I was at that dinner tonight had nothing to do with looking for another woman. I'm still trying to nail Kawowski down to a contract. He's the hardest deal maker I've ever encountered. He categorically refuses to admit he put out feelers to obtain the service we provide."

Joanna barely stopped herself from stamping her foot in frustration. Although she was to blame for this Kawowski thing in the first place, Rory took things to extreme lengths.

"I wanted to see how he operated," he went on. "I could hardly become one of his clients under my own name, and I needed to look a bit different. Otherwise I'd be playing into his hands." His mouth twisted self-mockingly. "I don't suppose you'll accept that. You won't accept anything I say."

He shrugged with an air of defeat and turned to Poppy, his hands gesturing an appeal for open-mindedness from her. Joanna was not about to let him get away with such blatant duplicity.

"That might have been how you came to be at the dinner, Rory," she conceded. "But that wasn't why you played up to Poppy. Or came home with her."

"Hold on, Joanna! Let's be fair about this," Poppy interjected on a critical note. "I'm sure Isaac liked me in my own right. I can feel that kind of thing, you know. And we were having such an interesting conversation—"

"His name is Rory!" Joanna snapped. "Isaac Stone does not exist! And while he's been flirting with you under an alias all night, he also had plans to meet me tomorrow. So you can see he believes in variety!"

Rory rolled his head to her with a sigh of exasperation. "You're being paranoid, Joanna. Why can't I be friends with Poppy? You obviously are, or you wouldn't be here."

"Inconvenient for you, isn't it, running into me at your new friend's home?" Joanna taunted.

"It doesn't inconvenience me at all. Though I am wondering what you're doing here. I thought you were living at home with your mother. That's why I sent the couriers there."

"They were redirected on," Poppy inserted, eager to be helpful in clearing up the misunderstanding. "Joanna's not living with her mother anymore."

Rory's face lit with interest. "Is that so?" He smiled encouragement at Poppy. "Since when?"

"She left her mother's home last Friday night. Over a week ago. I pressed her to stay with me until she was ready to move on."

Joanna fumed over Poppy's gullibility. One smile and Rory had her on a line, ready to be tugged in whenever it suited him.

"Well, I'm glad to hear she's finally cut free of her mother's influence," he said sanctimoniously. "I can tell you, Poppy, Fay Harding has been no friend to Joanna or me. She'd poison anything between us, given the chance."

Poppy at least had the grace to look uncomfortable at that claim, but she soldiered on, trying to be helpful. "Anyhow, it's all off with Brad. If you want to know."

"Poppy!" Joanna's steaming expostulation grabbed attention. "I'm quite capable of speaking for myself. I do not need you to give my ex-husband the private details of my life."

Poppy shrivelled on the spot, her face flushing with embarrassment over her indiscretion.

Rory, totally shameless as always, raised his eyebrows at Joanna in arch interest. "Worried about

Poppy telling me the truth, Joanna? Just for the record, did Brad have a change of heart or did you? Should I commiserate or congratulate?''

Joanna glared fierce scorn at him. "Instead of dishing out your spurious charm, why don't you tell Poppy the truth about Monique, Rory? Let her get this delightful evening with you in its proper perspective."

"Certainly!" he agreed. "Joanna might not have told you, Poppy, but I own and run a highly specialised market research company. Monique is one of my best people. And a good friend."

"And Rory sleeps with her," Joanna added with silky venom.

"Oh, Joanna!" He shook his head at her in weary disgust, then looked soulfully at Poppy. "It's this kind of accusation that broke up our marriage. Joanna doesn't bother asking me for the truth. She prefers to believe the worst of me."

"That's not true!" Joanna cried indignantly. If he thought he could bamboozle her as he had bamboozled Brad, he could think again! Monique had been too intimately familiar with Rory's home for Joanna to believe she was no more than a Platonic friend in a working relationship with Rory.

"Then why slander both me and Monique when we were only trying to help you?" Rory demanded as though he was as pure as driven snow. "Just because you've decided you don't want Brad..." He cocked a taunting eyebrow. "Or was it the other way around? The woman scorned, Joanna? Despite my efforts, and

Monique's, to keep your character pearly white, Brad persisted in thinking the worst of you?''

"No, he didn't! *I* broke it off, if you must know."

"Oh? Why?" His eyes gleamed satisfaction. "You found he couldn't match what we had together?"

The allusion to their "dirty" afternoon sent a wave of burning shame through Joanna. Rory had seduced her into believing the impossible might be possible.

"Does everything come down to sex with you, Rory?" She shot a hard look at Poppy. "Did I tell you the woman Rory got pregnant was one of his employees? She, too, was helping him with his market research. No doubt she thought he was friendly and sympathetic. And he had his way with her while I was with my mother, where he thought I'd be tonight."

She looked at Rory, whose face had tightened into a grim mask. It struck no cautionary note in Joanna. The pain of desecrated dreams kept pumping bitter distrust through her mind.

"How many others were there, Rory? The ones that didn't get pregnant. Do you make a habit of going around your whole staff? Bernice. Monique. Where does it end?"

"It ends right here, Joanna," he said quietly.

"Fine!" she snapped. "Then I'll show you to the door and save Poppy the trouble."

"No, thank you. I've already been through that once with you, Joanna. I came with Poppy. She can show me to the door when she wants to. Perhaps her mind isn't as full of closed doors as yours is."

"Do as you please with anyone you please," Joanna seethed at him. Her eyes glittered a savage warning at

Poppy. "Don't blame me if Rory Grayson takes you for a ride. Because that's all it will be, I promise you."

She swept out of the room in high dudgeon.

"What a bewitching woman!" Rory drawled in sardonic admiration. Then with more bite, "Takes after her mother. She was a witch, too."

Joanna marched into her temporary bedroom and slammed the door shut behind her as a mark of severing all connection with the whole scene. And its consequences! She had done her best to remove the wool from Poppy's eyes. If her friend wanted to be a Rory Grayson victim, on her head be it!

She threw off her clothes, dragged on her pyjamas, got into bed and pulled the pillow over her head to block out the low murmurs coming through the wall from the living room. She had made a stupid mistake in seeing Rory again, then compounded it by showing she was still vulnerable to the attraction between them. Well, she knew for certain now that he couldn't be trusted out of her sight.

Bernice, she could have forgiven. Monique was understandable. But this coming home with Poppy proved she had been right to divorce him. And she wasn't going to grieve this time. She would make something positive of her life if it killed her!

She would leave here tomorrow, find a room somewhere and not tell anyone where she was. After all, she had done everything she could for Poppy. It was time to bow out and be on her way. Wherever that might be.

The murmurs went on for a long time. Joanna could not help wondering what they were talking about.

Blocking out the murmurs with her pillow didn't help Joanna to any peace of mind, either. Would Rory be so crass as to kiss Poppy? Make love to her? Joanna writhed in revulsion at the thought.

It was an enormous relief when she heard movement down the hallway to the front door, followed by the sounds of departure. Finally silence reigned. The torment of Rory's intrusive presence slowly fragmented into the oblivion of sleep.

It was another day when she awoke. A day of action, she promised herself. When she trailed out to the kitchenette for her first morning cup of coffee, she found Poppy seated on one of the stools, sipping at the cup of tea in her hand as she idly perused the Sunday newspaper spread out on the counter. She gave Joanna a wary look as she said, "Good morning."

"Is it good?" Joanna replied flippantly, hiding the flutter of nerves that was wreaking havoc with her stomach. She couldn't be so stupid as to feel jealous of Poppy, yet she hated the fact that Rory had stayed talking to her for so long. "I'll be moving on today, Poppy," she blurted out as she busied herself with making the coffee.

"Because of last night?" Poppy asked quietly.

"I don't want to cramp your style. If you're going to see Rory again..."

"I'm not, Joanna."

"But you said you had a marvellous time with him," she argued in some crazy spirit of perversity.

"I did. It was the best night of my life."

"Well, don't let me stop you from enjoying yourself with him. After all, he's a free agent."

"I don't think so."

"You mean—" Joanna gritted her teeth, then bit out the words "—because of Monique?"

"No. It's what you said yesterday, Joanna, about divorced people being damaged. Rory Grayson isn't free of you. He likes me, but it's you he wants."

Joanna went absolutely still except for her heart. For some mad reason of its own, it careered around her chest with painful force. "Want isn't love," she said flatly.

"He cares about you, Joanna," Poppy said softly. "He wouldn't have said or done the things he did if he didn't care."

Joanna spun around to face her friend. "What things?"

Poppy met her gaze levelly. "You know. He cared enough to try to win you back when you went to see him."

"He told you that?"

"Not exactly. I asked him to explain what you were referring to in front of me last night."

"No doubt he gave a virtuous version."

"No more than a brief outline, Joanna. Enough for me to realise he cared about your happiness with Brad if that was what you wanted. And do you think sending the money and then the invitation to lunch is the action of a man who doesn't care?"

"You don't understand, Poppy. It's all a game to Rory. A matter of ego," Joanna said cynically.

Poppy shook her head. "I think he's reacting against hurt the same as you are, Joanna."

"Did you tell you that?" she scoffed.

"He didn't have to."

"Did he pour his bleeding heart out to you after I went to bed?"

"He didn't have to."

Poppy looked at her in a measuring way that made Joanna ashamed of her sarcasm, but somehow she couldn't take it back. When she remained stubbornly silent, Poppy offered more of her impression of Rory as food for thought.

"He doesn't strike me as the kind of man to weep on a woman's shoulder. More the type to offer a shoulder to a weeping woman." She gave a crooked little smile. "At least that was more or less what he did for me."

Joanna frowned. "What do you mean?"

"He didn't want to talk about you, but he didn't want to leave, either. Not straightaway. Whether it was a matter of pride, or giving you a chance to rethink, I don't know. He encouraged me to talk about my dreams. I found him very sympathetic and helpful."

"Rory always was a good listener," Joanna conceded grudgingly.

"I think basically he's a very kind and caring person. Not in a shallow conventional way, but digging right down to the heart of what really matters. He invites honesty because he's so self-knowingly honest himself."

"Poppy, he was pumping you for information he could use to prove his case to Kawowski. You don't understand how Rory's mind works."

Poppy heaved a defeated sigh. "If you say so, Joanna. In any event, I assure you he won't be coming back here, so there's no need for you to rush off."

Joanna shook her head. It troubled her that Poppy's perceptions might be correct. It would mean she had made terrible mistakes, different ones to what she had thought last night, mistakes so costly they didn't bear thinking about.

Besides, Poppy had only known Rory for one night. How could first impressions measure up against the hard evidence of her own experiences with him? Rory might be honest, ruthlessly honest about some things, *but he had cheated on her!*

To be completely fair, Joanna wondered if the emotional trauma that had ended their marriage had affected her so much she had become too extreme in her judgements. Maybe she should reassess. Yet what was the point? It was almost certainly too late.

She looked at her friend with hopeless, helpless eyes. "I have to go. I'm sorry, Poppy, but I can't stay here anymore. It's like with my mother. You know too much. Even if we don't talk about him, it will be there between us. And I need to get away from Rory."

"Do you, Joanna?" Poppy asked gently. "Or do you need to be with him?"

Joanna couldn't bear to face the need Rory had reawakened in her last week. "How do you begin to trust someone when they've shown they cannot be trusted?" she cried despairingly.

Sadness dulled the hope in Poppy's eyes. "I'm sorry, Joanna. I wish I could help. You've been so good to me."

Joanna managed a wobbly smile. "Stay good. No backsliding to French pastries."

Poppy forced a smile, responding to Joanna's need to lighten the mood between them. "Don't worry. I'm now determined to go after what I want for myself."

Rory wasn't mentioned again.

Later that morning Joanna packed her suitcase and took a taxi to a private hotel that catered to permanent guests. It was situated in easy walking distance of the North Sydney railway station. As stopgap accommodation until she was in work again, it was relatively cheap and handy to the three workplaces on her list of job applications.

Now I can break free of the past, Joanna thought, closing herself into the somewhat drab but adequately furnished bed-sitting room. But no amount of positive thinking could take the chill off her loneliness.

Unbidden, yet with irresistible force, the rooms of her dream home—hers and Rory's dream home— drifted into her mind and lingered there, each perfect detail remembered lovingly, achingly.

If Rory had done it for her ...

If he still cared ...

What if Poppy was right, and Rory hurt over her as much as she did over him? Was there any way of reaching across the chasm of hurt and once again being right for each other?

Not now, she decided listlessly. Maybe if she had stayed with Rory last Friday night instead of going with Brad ... Or if she had been prepared to listen to him last night... But there would always be that deep, dark abyss of hurt that they would never be ablc to erase. It would distort things, colour things differently, rise up to hang like a storm cloud over any happiness they might achieve.

Let it go, Joanna recited in feverish desperation. Let it go.

CHAPTER TEN

JOANNA POSTED the job applications first thing on Monday morning. To her immense relief and gratification she received replies to all three, formally asking her to attend interviews the following week. While an interview was no guarantee of getting employment, Joanna was determined to do her best to impress.

When Saturday came, she combed through the positions-vacant columns in the newspapers, marking out more possibilities. She couldn't afford to take success for granted. There might be more suitable applicants than herself being interviewed, as well. She wrote an application for a job in the travel industry and a letter of inquiry to a company that offered tutoring to slow students.

She also looked up adult education courses to see what was on offer. She found the loneliness of the nights very hard to bear. If she took some evening classes, met a new crowd of people, maybe her life wouldn't feel quite so empty.

On the other hand, it was sensible to wait until she was settled in a job first. She didn't know which college would be most convenient to attend until she decided where to live. She certainly wasn't going to stay in this private hotel forever.

Joanna's confidence in achieving what she wanted was severely dented by the end of her third week of independence. At the conclusion of each job interview she was told, "We'll let you know," but nobody let her know anything. She was not even given the courtesy of being told she was rejected, just left hoping and waiting until hope wilted.

Added to this build-up of tension was another worry that grew as each day passed, as what should be happening showed no sign of doing so. Joanna tried telling herself it was too unreasonable for her to get pregnant in one single afternoon with Rory when she had tried for six full months to conceive his baby without result. Life couldn't be that unfair to her. It would be the ultimate irony.

Why hadn't she thought of the danger? It was no excuse that she had become accustomed to Brad taking contraceptive precautions whenever it had been necessary. Rory would have undoubtedly assumed she was on the pill if she was going to marry Brad. If she was ruthlessly honest, the plain truth was she hadn't wanted to think about what she was doing. She had wanted to be carried away on the tide of passion Rory had stirred.

Steeling herself to put the matter beyond doubt instead of waiting and worrying about it, Joanna bought a test kit from a chemist shop. The result was unequivocally positive. She was pregnant.

Joanna had known many lonely moments in her life, but this was the loneliest. It was the worst possible time for her to have a baby. She had no job, no partner to support her, no help, no security behind her. She could not, would not go back to her mother. Not having Rory's baby. And it wouldn't be fair to ask her sister for anything. That would also invite their mother's unrelenting disapproval.

She was on her own.

Unless Rory... Could she go to him? Did he still want her? Did he really care for her? Would he love their baby? Was this a chance for them to come together again and make something good of the future for the sake of their child? Or was that clutching at straws?

Joanna agonised over what to do for a full twenty-four hours before coming to a decision. It was Rory's child as well as hers. He was at least entitled to know about it. How he chose to react to the news was up to him.

Joanna inwardly writhed over the memory of her bitter taunt to him about casual bed mates and fathering children she didn't know about. If he laughed in her face now, and told her to have a convenient miscarriage, that was surely the worst he could do to her, the absolute bottom line of the down side.

Countering that was a range of possibilities that Joanna hoped might eventuate. The only way to find out was to go to Rory in person and face whatever happened then. Figuring that he should be home at nine o'clock on a Saturday morning, she screwed her courage to the highest pitch of resolution and made a telephone call to his home.

One buzz... two, three, four.

Her heart quailed as an image of Rory and Monique, tangled in bed together, flashed into her mind. If a female voice answered the telephone, she would hang up.

"Rory Grayson."

Hearing *his* voice paralysed Joanna for a moment.

"Hello?" Rory prompted.

"It's Joanna." The words spilled out with no set purpose to follow them.

There was a brief, nerve-tearing silence before Rory's voice came again, making a matter-of-fact inquiry. "What can I do for you, Joanna?"

"Have I caught you at a bad time?" she asked.

A pause. "Not really," he drawled.

She forced out the necessary request. "May I come and see you this morning?"

Another pause.

"It's important," she pressed.

"Of course. It would have to be," he said in a tone that would have withered the fresh shoots of spring leaves. "Come whenever you like."

Too late... The words beat a death knell in her heart. She had rejected his appeal for her belief in him once too often that night at Poppy's. He didn't want to see her again. He no longer cared.

Yet there was still the baby to consider.

"I'll come straightaway then," she said, desperate to get it over and done with.

She hung up before he could make any further comment, if he'd had a mind to. Having used a public telephone box outside the North Sydney railway station, she wasted no time in walking down to the taxi rank that served train commuters. A number of cabs waited there. She climbed into the first, gave Rory's address in Dee Why and sat in a state of numb suspension throughout the trip.

It seemed to take Rory aeons to answer his doorbell, although it was probably only a minute or two. Joanna had rehearsed a multitude of opening lines, but when he stood in front of her, none of them seemed appropriate. His dark blue jeans and red pullover emphasised his strong masculinity, evoking memories of how she had become pregnant.

Her lack of greeting brought a cynical twist to his mouth. His gaze flicked over the jade jumpsuit she wore, selected more for its comfortable warmth than stylishness. She felt the cold today. When his eyes met hers again there was a wintry lack of warmth in them.

"Do you want to come in or not, Joanna?"

"Yes. Please," she said stiffly.

He stood back and beckoned her forward. She stepped past him as quickly as she could and plunged almost blindly on to the living room, conscious of him closing the door behind her, conscious of having to face him with a fact that he couldn't possibly want to hear. She needed space around her before she did that. Distance between them. But her headlong rush came to a stumbling halt when she saw Monique coming in from the terrace, Monique in black silk lounging pyjamas.

Then a man appeared beside her, a genial giant of a man who slid a possessive arm around Monique's waist and raised his other hand in greeting to Joanna.

"Hi!" he said with a grin. "I'm Isaac Stone. Monique's pet husband. And we're just going."

Confusion whirled through Joanna's mind. What was really happening? Surely nobody in the world was called Isaac Stone! Was this another terrible deception? Some kind of set-up to justify something? She clutched at the one essential fact.

"You're Monique's husband?" she queried.

"Hundreds of witnesses at the wedding," he affirmed cheerfully. "She made me do it. Five years ago today. Feels like five minutes."

"But that's not the only good news," Rory said.

"No, indeed!" Isaac Stone boomed with huge good humour. He hugged Monique more closely to him and dropped a kiss on her riotous curls. "My darling wife is giving me a baby. Oh, what a marvellous, magnificent, absolutely scintillatingly glorious day it is today!"

Joanna's stomach cramped with a dreadful hollow feeling. This was how it should be with the news of a baby. But it couldn't be for her and Rory. And once again she felt cheated of what should have been. Were none of her dreams ever to be fulfilled with the happiness they had once promised?

Monique's face glowed at her husband with the luminous beauty of deep inner happiness. "That's not all, Isaac. You've left something very important out. Tell Joanna what you've done."

He shook his head. "That's nothing, my love."

"You're too modest. If you won't tell Joanna, I will." She turned to Joanna with shining eyes. "I'm so proud of him. He won one of the most prestigious awards in Australia for one of his paintings. And amongst the prizes is a trip to Paris for two, so he can study at the great art museums there."

This was no play-acting. These were two people so genuinely in love that even a blind person could feel it. "That's wonderful!" Joanna said, but she was devastatingly aware of how wrongly she had judged Monique. And Rory.

"Ah, it's all very well to have my work publicly acclaimed now," Isaac said dryly, "but it was Rory who believed in my talent when no-one else did. He kept me going by buying my paintings." His big, genial face beamed warm gratitude at Rory. "I'll never be able to thank you enough for having that faith in me. It gave me faith in myself."

Rory shook his head. "Your waterlilies painting is a masterpiece, Isaac. I bought it too cheaply."

Joanna vividly recalled the painting over Rory's bed. It explained Monique's familiarity with his bedroom. And home. Particularly since she and her husband were both close friends of his.

For the first time, Joanna noticed the rings on Monique's left hand. If only she had seen those... No, it would only have confirmed to her that adultery meant nothing to Rory. He was right. She didn't know when she had first started doing it, but she had been thinking the worst of him for a long time now.

"Well, we must go!" Monique declared. "Thank you for the champagne breakfast, Rory. Thanks for the celebration."

"My pleasure," he said warmly.

Isaac scooped Monique forward with him, his exuberance returning at the thought of having his wife to himself. The huge disparity of their respective physiques was dwarfed by the strength of the bond between them. As they drew level with Joanna, Monique broke away from Isaac to press an impulsive kiss on Joanna's cheek.

"I hope you'll know the happiness I feel today, Joanna," she said, looking into her eyes as though she was trying to give her another message, this time unspoken.

It filled Joanna with acute embarrassment but she managed to say, "Thank you."

Isaac bestowed a benevolent smile on Joanna as he tucked his wife to his side again. "We happen to be Rory's neighbours, as well as friends. Hope we see you again sometime, Joanna."

"Yes," she murmured weakly.

They left.

Alone with Rory, Joanna found herself more tongue-tied than before. Guilt added its heavy weight to her despair, making any appeal for another chance utterly impossible.

"You'll have to excuse Monique and Isaac. They're both romantics," Rory said dryly. He gave a harsh little laugh. "Monique would die if she knew what interpretation you put on her impromptu visit with the champagne the other week. The bottle was for us, believe it or not. To celebrate our getting together again."

"I'm sorry," Joanna blurted out, her eyes begging him to believe her apology. "For what I thought. And said," she added, hating the hard cynicism that looked back at her, but unable to blame him for it.

He shrugged. "Par for the course with you, isn't it, Joanna?" He waved to the leather couches. "Would you like to sit down, or won't you be staying that long?"

His dismissive tone emphasised the disinterest expressed in his words. His invitation to sit was so carelessly given that Joanna could not accept it, despite the weakness that made her legs feel unsteady.

"I suppose it's now irrelevant that I deeply regret how I've behaved towards you since I left here that night," she said in dull resignation.

His mouth curled. "A prick of conscience, Joanna? What a pity you came in on Monique and Isaac! You could have gone on hating me with all your justification intact."

"I don't hate you, Rory."

His eyes glittered a mocking challenge, but before she could think of any words that might convince him, he turned away and strolled across the room to the doors that led onto the terrace. He did not step outside. He stood on the threshold looking out to sea, his profile outlined by bright sunlight that threw his darkly brooding face into sharp relief.

She saw his chest expand as he filled his lungs with fresh, salty air. She had the impression that to him it was cleansing air. When he spoke it was in a dull monotone, addressed to the view of sand and sea.

"There comes a time in everybody's life when the inevitable has to be faced. It's possible to love someone with every atom of one's being, but being with them, or living with them, is simply impossible. Love turns to hate. And anger. And despair.''

Joanna knew, with a dreadful sense of hollowness, that he was not speaking of her, but of himself.

''There comes a time when all personal resources have been exhausted,'' he continued. ''When enough is too much, and there's nothing more to give. When trying to attain the impossible is an exercise in futility. That point was probably reached between us a long time ago. Perhaps long before you divorced me. The ground had to have already been laid for what happened.''

His head turned slowly towards her, as though he was reluctant to acknowledge her presence in his home. She understood why when she saw the pain etched on his face, the hurt in his eyes. It was she who had put it there.

''But I had my dreams and I didn't want to let go,'' he went on. ''Now I realise those dreams can never be fulfilled. That beating against hope is like hitting a brick wall. And I feel empty, drained, exhausted, inadequate—'' his mouth twisted into a self-mocking grimace ''—and stupid for even trying.''

She knew that to say she was sorry would be utterly meaningless. There were no words that could reach across this unbridgeable chasm, no answer she could give. If she threw herself into his arms and said she loved him and tried to gentle away the pain, he wouldn't believe her.

He lifted one hand in a spiritless gesture of concession. ''You can ask me anything you like and you can have it, Joanna. But I never want to see you again. I want the peace of being . . . alone."

She understood that, too, and wished she didn't have to say what she had come to say. For a moment she considered walking away without telling him about the baby, but their unborn child had rights that she couldn't ignore. Left with no choice but to come straight to the point, Joanna did her best to formulate the necessary words in her shattered mind.

"What I have to say won't take very long," she assured him huskily. "I think you have the right to know I'm carrying your baby."

Shock and disbelief tightened into anger. His eyes stabbed bitter contempt at her. "What petty revenge is this, Joanna? A savage little twist on the past? Fabricating the same claim that the woman who killed off our marriage made on me?"

Now he's doing to me what I once did to him, Joanna thought in wretched misery. When I need his support most, he won't give it.

"That's all I came to tell you," she stated flatly. "Whether you believe it or not, it's true."

"Oh, for God's sake!" he exploded. "What do you expect me to believe? That you conveniently forgot to take the pill for a few days before you came to see me? That you took precautions with Brad but not with me?"

Joanna flinched at the savage mockery in his voice. A sting of pride urged her to leave, yet some innate sense of fairness demanded that she answer the accusation. "Brad and I had sex so infrequently that I wasn't on the pill. He used a condom."

"Then why didn't you ask me to use one?"

"I didn't think of it."

Burning bitterness seared her as Rory repeated, "You didn't think of it!"

She ignored the scorching heat in her cheeks. She owed him the truth and gave it. "I never told you this, but for the last six months before we separated, I was trying to conceive. It never happened. I wasn't even sure that we could have children together."

"Well, maybe we can't," he drawled. "Condoms aren't one hundred percent effective. When did you last have sex with Brad?"

She stared at him in blank shock, not having foreseen this possibility amongst the range of reactions she might get from Rory. She was too appalled to form any reply.

Rory broke into harsh, derisive laughter. "Don't tell me you've forgotten I've been through this before. Maybe I'm fated to have women loading another man's child on me. But, of course, you didn't believe I was innocent of that charge, did you? No standing by her man from Joanna Harding. Not when he needed it most. Just condemn him out of hand and cut him dead."

Had he been innocent? Joanna's reeling mind fought against accepting that. It would be the most damning mistake of all!

"Perhaps it serves your warped sense of justice to hang Brad's child on me, too," Rory ranted on. "Especially since you probably hate yourself for having sex with me. Is that it, Joanna? The ultimate knife in the heart?"

She couldn't take any more. Whatever the rights and wrongs between them, this was definitely the end. She wrapped herself in protective dignity and delivered her last judgement on Rory Grayson.

"If you'd wanted to, you could have proved your paternity with a DNA test. But it's all so dirty, and ugly, and sordid, I'd prefer you to believe the child is Brad's. That way you never have to see either of us, and you have your wish . . . to be alone."

She forced her legs to take her out of his apartment, out of his life forever. He made no attempt to stop her, not by word or action. The elevator was waiting. She stepped into it like a sleepwalker, anaesthetised to any hard realities. It took her down to street level. She walked out of the building, too shattered to feel anything, too exhausted to care.

She spotted a bus-stop on the other side of the road. It was something to head for. She stepped off the sidewalk. In her preoccupation, she hadn't noticed the oncoming vehicle. A screaming of brakes alerted Joanna to the danger.

Why her feet propelled her towards the centre line Joanna did not know, but by some lucky miracle the car swerved towards the sidewalk. She felt a hot rush of wind as it almost grazed her in passing. An angry male voice yelled, "You crazy bitch!" then followed it with a string of profanities.

Other cars squealed to abrupt halts, skewed across the road, blocking lanes. *What have I done?* Joanna thought desperately, her whole body tensing in expectant horror as she waited for the crunch of metal to confirm a ghastly pile-up.

It did not come.

Nothing seemed to be hitting anything else, but the road was jammed across all lanes as drivers took evasive action from the blockage in front of them. Men and women were leaping out of their vehicles, shaking their fists at her. A babble of angry voices rose in curses and accusations. Joanna's head started swimming in sickening circles. She wished the ground would open up and swallow her. Her knees started to buckle.

Then she saw Rory, swinging himself across the yellow bonnet of a car, running towards her at a frantic pace. She tried to say, *I didn't mean it,* but her voice wasn't working. Her body gave up on her, as well. She felt herself falling, but her collapse towards the pavement was halted by strong hands grabbing her under her arms, supporting her, lifting her.

Somewhere in the whirling haze of her mind she knew it was Rory who picked her up, Rory whose arms held her closely cradled to the heaving warmth of his chest. She felt safe there. It seemed easy to close her eyes and let her head rest against his shoulder.

An irate, abusive crowd of people gathered around them. She heard Rory cut them short with imperious authority. "Don't be a pack of hyenas! Can't you see the woman's not well? She's pregnant. She needs medical help."

The yelling died to a mutter.

"Make way!" Rory commanded.

There was a shuffle of movement. A siren sounded in the distance. Rory's footsteps crunched loudly on the asphalt as he carried her with him, away from the centre of trouble.

Joanna kept her eyes closed. She did not want to know what was happening, only that Rory was holding her close. She didn't want that to change.

CHAPTER ELEVEN

JOANNA WAS vaguely aware of a siren whooping louder and louder. Then there were more car doors banging, and another commotion started around them. She burrowed her head into the curve of Rory's neck and shoulder and willed the rest of the world to go away. She felt too weak to cope with it right now. Besides, only one thing mattered. Rory had come after her. He was supporting her, protecting her, giving her what she needed.

"Hold it right there!" a voice bellowed. "You're not leaving the scene of this accident!"

"Officer, if you need me, you know where to find me," Rory declared. "The lady will be there, too. And I want you to be the first to know. I'm going to be a father."

"Are you now? Well, I'll be damned! Thought she went off with the other bloke. Wasn't she going to marry him?"

"That's all changed, Officer. And I'd like to thank you for your help and understanding in the matter."

Joanna cautiously cocked one eye open. The same two policemen who had come to Rory's apartment were surveying the scene with interest. A lady with a blue rinse plucked at the larger policeman's arm and archly told him, "She's pregnant. That explains everything."

"And she needs to lie down and be pampered," Rory said firmly. He raised his voice. "I've got a precious bundle here. Will everyone make way?"

Joanna wondered which was the precious bundle, her or the baby, but now was not the time to raise questions.

Rory moved on. Apart from shot nerves and frayed tempers, no harm had been done to anyone or anything, and the angry mood had dissipated. People clapped Rory's back and offered well wishes and congratulations. He had turned the whole situation around. Again.

Joanna half expected Rory to make some inquiry of her well-being once he left the crowd behind, but he bore her weight in silence all the way up to his apartment. She said no word, either, aware of how fragile this peace might be between them. If Rory's concern was only for the baby whom he now seemed to accept as his, waiting for his next move seemed the wisest course of action.

He took her straight into his bedroom and laid her gently on the bed. When he withdrew his hold on her, Joanna felt such a sharp bereftness that she had to grit her teeth to stop from crying out a protest. Her eyes flew open, anxious to catch the expression on his face, to gain some clue on what he was really feeling.

The strain of carrying her so far was evident in his heavy breathing and the flexing of his shoulders. His show of good humour with the policeman had obviously only been that. A show. The grim set of his mouth and weariness of spirit dulling his blue eyes hardly assured Joanna of any joy in his fatherhood. The hope she had nursed while in his arms started to wilt.

"Stay there!" he commanded. "I'll get you a cup of tea."

Joanna felt too limp to move anyway. It had been a hellish morning and didn't look like improving despite Rory's having come to her rescue. She lay on the bed she had made for herself in succumbing to the personal gratification of knowing Rory again, and listlessly wondered what could be salvaged from the wreckage of their love for each other.

Rory returned with the cup of tea, which he placed on the bedside table. He made no attempt to help her drink it. He drew a chair up to easy conversational distance from the bed and dropped into it with an air of determined patience. His eyes held a guarded watchfulness that gave nothing away.

Joanna hitched herself up on the pillows and sipped at the tea, needing to replenish her strength to face another encounter with him. "What changed your mind, Rory?" she asked when she found his silence too oppressive to let it continue.

"You may be screwed up in many ways, Joanna, but underneath whatever misconceptions and prejudices you have, there's a hard core of integrity." He gave her a half smile that was loaded with irony. "That's why you dumped me. Integrity is very important to you. It took me a few minutes to remember that. Then I realised that no matter what you felt about me, the child had to be mine."

"And you care about that?"

"I am human," he said self-mockingly. "I always did want children with you, Joanna. I wish..." He shrugged and leaned forward, forearms resting on his thighs, head bowed. "No point in going over what didn't happen. It's happened now." He raised half-hooded eyes. "Have you thought out what you want to do?"

"I only found out yesterday," she temporised, wary of inviting more rejection from him.

"I guess it came as a shock," he said gently.

The unexpected softness from him brought a blur of tears to Joanna's eyes. "Yes," she acknowledged, quickly turning aside to swallow some more tea. "Thank you for helping me out of that mess in the street," she added belatedly.

"The least I could do," he muttered. "I'm sorry for saying all I did before. It couldn't have come at a worse time for you."

The deep throb of regret in his voice gave her the courage to meet his eyes again. "I haven't treated you all that well, either, Rory," she said softly. Then with a half-smile at him, "I screwed up everything as badly as I possibly could."

"Difficult to deprogram something set in concrete," he said, not unsympathetically. "Given what you believe about me cheating on you when we were married, the rest follows fairly reasonably."

"Didn't you cheat on me, Rory?" Her chest felt unbearably tight as she waited for his answer.

"I know you felt cheated of many things, Joanna," he replied quietly. "But I was never unfaithful to you.

Not with that woman or with anyone else. I didn't want any other woman."

The pain of that time clutched at Joanna's heart. She couldn't help but question Rory's claim, even now. "Then why did she say it was you who made her pregnant?"

He shook his head. "Only she can tell you why, Joanna. For whatever reason she had, she picked on me and stuck to her story as though she couldn't let herself accept anything else."

"It makes no sense."

He sighed, then gave her a look so bleak it chilled her soul. "What good does it do, going over this again, Joanna?"

She lowered her eyes, struggling to be pragmatic about the situation. She would lose everything she'd gained with Rory if she continued in this strain. Whatever the truth of the past, it was the future that had to concern her now. And not only for her own sake. Besides, Poppy was right. She *needed* to be with Rory.

Despite the importance of the question and his response to it, she couldn't bring herself to look at him as she asked, "What do you want, Rory, now that you know about the baby?"

Silence. A tense, weighted silence that seemed to hold both their futures and the future of their child in the balance. Joanna waited, dreading Rory's reply, yet agonised by the uncertainty of her position.

"Would you consider marrying me again, Joanna?"

Her eyes flew to his in tortured disbelief. He couldn't mean it! Not after what he'd said before. Yet he held her gaze with a steadiness of purpose that assured her it was a serious proposition.

"Yes."

She heard herself whisper the fateful word, a bare breath of sound that had streaked out of the pulsing need in her heart and spilled from her lips without any conscious decision from her mind.

"Is that fear speaking, Joanna, or do you want to try to make it work for us?" Rory asked softly. "If it's for the sake of the child—"

"No." Her eyes begged his belief. "For all three of us, Rory."

He nodded. A gleam of understanding appeared in his eyes. "You always did whatever you decided to do with your whole heart."

Joanna took a deep breath and asked, "What about your heart, Rory?"

His mouth twisted. "If we're getting married, I'd prefer you not to keep teaching at Brad's school. It might be an unliberated attitude, but that doesn't sit well with me. You might start making comparisons I wouldn't like to live with."

"I'm not there anymore. I resigned the night I broke off with Brad."

Rory raised his eyebrows. "Big break. Your mother, Brad and your job all in one night?"

"I guess you could say you brought things to a head, Rory."

"But you didn't want me back."

She gave a grimace that was half appeal, half apology. "Yes, I did. But not with Monique."

His face tightened. He turned his gaze aside, looking out to the glittering horizon of sea and sky that could be seen through the wall of glass at the end of the room.

"So what's your present situation? Are you at a new school? Still living with Poppy?"

"No. I took a room in a private hotel after that night you came to Poppy's. And I haven't been able to get a job. Any job," she added with painful honesty, knowing he must think she had come to him out of sheer desperation.

She saw a muscle contract in his cheek. Slowly, very slowly, he turned to face her again. There was a glitter of mockery in his eyes. "Well, at least it's something that you came to me instead of going back to your mother."

She flushed. "I didn't intend asking you for help, Rory. I would have managed alone if—"

"Forget it," he interrupted firmly. "We'll make a go of it together, Joanna, come what may."

But there was not the joy in having decided to remarry that there should have been. Rory's dispassionate mood kept discussion of the situation along practical lines. Whenever painful subjects were touched upon, they both retreated quickly, not wanting to air the wounds that had been fully exposed this morning. By tacit consent they drew a veil over the past and concentrated solely on plans for the future.

Rory produced a salad and some fresh bread rolls for lunch. Neither of them had much appetite, but both made an effort to establish the normality of eating, as though this was any other day and not the most momentous day in their lives.

It was a relief to Joanna when Rory suggested she spend the afternoon resting in bed while he collected her things from the hotel and settled her accommodation account there. The strain of being careful of each other's feelings was beginning to tell on both of them, with tense little silences separating the attempts to negotiate suitable and sensible arrangements. It will get better, she assured herself. All they needed was a period of adjustment. Hadn't Rory proved the magic was still there for them?

It wasn't dead.

It couldn't be dead.

She wouldn't let it be dead.

All she had to do was reach out to Rory, and it would spring alive again. Yet somehow that proved more difficult than Joanna could have imagined.

Having had little sleep the night before, and exhausted from this morning's traumatic events, Joanna slept most of the afternoon away. When she awoke she found she could not cross the distance that Rory kept between them. He had brought all her things from the hotel and had made room for them in his closets and cupboards, but despite the kind consideration he showed her, there was a diffidence in his manner that did not invite touching. Fear of rejection made Joanna feel increasingly inhibited, especially since he showed no inclination to touch her himself.

All evening she had the feeling of walking on eggshells, where any step forward might crack the truce between them. Rory took her to a restaurant in the neighbouring beach suburb of Manly. They shared a candlelit dinner, which could have been romantic, given the right kind of rapport between them. Try as she might, Joanna could not establish anything more intimate than the most superficially polite conversation.

She asked him about his business. That seemed safe. Until he dryly remarked that at least money shouldn't be a problem between them this time around. He went on to say he would open a bank account for her on Monday and she didn't have to be accountable to anyone for whatever she spent. He wanted her to have economic freedom.

"I'm not marrying you for your money, Rory," she blurted out, desperate to clear away any reservation he might have about her on that score.

He looked surprised. "I know that, Joanna."

"Then why..." She gestured helplessly, unable to express the indefinable barrier he seemed to have built around himself.

"Marriage is about sharing one's worldly goods, isn't it?" he said, his eyes issuing a cool challenge. "Do you have some objection to accepting from me what you once gave?"

"No," she said in a small voice, chillingly aware that he was redressing the debt from their first marriage, a debt that he had twice tried to pay.

Did he have some balance sheet in his mind that had to be evened up before he could accept her back into his life? Joanna had the sinking feeling that she would never finish atoning for the rejections she had given him. They would come back to haunt her again and again, regardless of how right she had felt about them when she had handed them out.

As she lay in the darkness beside Rory that night, Joanna had more time to contemplate the impulsive decision she had made to stay with him. He had not kissed her good-night, let alone made the slightest overture that could be interpreted as a desire to make love. They were in the same bed but they might as well have been a million miles apart.

Was he thinking about her intimacy with Brad? That hadn't stopped him from wanting her for a dirty weekend, Joanna reasoned frantically. Was he brooding over her accusations about Monique? Did he still feel drained of all feeling, as he had described this morning? If so, what could she do to change that? Or was it too late?

Her body was rigid with torment, aching to roll over and curl up against his. She needed him, wanted his loving so much, yet she could not bring herself to make the move, not without some encouragement from him. And none came.

Joanna hated the luxurious space of the perfectly sprung king-size bed. She fiercely wished they were back in the old double bed that had been one of the banes of their married life. The sag in its middle had made it impossible for them to sleep apart. They had always ended up tangled together, even on the hottest nights of the year.

Rory was right, she decided bitterly. Having the money to enjoy every material comfort didn't compensate for what was missing. How long would this estrangement go on? Was Rory testing her commitment to their remarriage by keeping their relationship non-sexual for a while? Was it some kind of punishment for her thinking the worst of him?

For all her tortured thoughts, Joanna was none the wiser when she finally drifted into sleep. She did not feel any more enlightened the next morning, either. Rory was gone from the bed when she awoke.

After she had washed and tidied herself, she found him on the terrace outside the bedroom. The cane table was already set for breakfast, and a pot of coffee stood waiting. They exchanged polite greetings, their eyes skating over each other, not lingering.

Rory insisted on serving her coffee. Joanna walked over to the railing, too restless to sit down. She tried to enjoy the sunshine and the view of the sea. It was a fine morning. In other circumstances she would have called it a beautiful morning, but it didn't *feel* beautiful. There was no sense of sharing it with Rory.

He handed her the coffee and asked what she would like for breakfast. She thought if he spoke to her once more in that polite, impersonal voice, she would scream. Driven by the need to smash at least one barrier, Joanna grasped his arm and lifted openly pleading eyes to his.

"I want you to know, Rory, I rarely compared you and Brad. There was good reason for it. Whenever I did think of you when I was with Brad, Brad always came off worse."

"Quite a dilemma for you, Joanna," he said dryly, his eyes mocking her attempt to put things right between them.

"That was why I had to come and see you that day. If I was to marry Brad..."

"Do you still like your eggs poached?"

"Damn it! Don't cut me off like this!"

Joanna bit down on her rising temper as she released his arm and turned to set her cup of coffee on the table. Her hand was shaking. She sucked in a deep breath, aware that anger would probably lose her everything. When she faced him again, she was once more the petitioner, begging his understanding.

"Rory, I'm trying to tell you about my feelings. That one afternoon with you, and the marriage with Brad was off. The horrible things I said to you, the horrible, cutting words, were due to the injury to my pride in still wanting you. I took it out on you."

"I know that, Joanna," he said impassively.

She wasn't getting through at all. Her words seemed meaningless to him, spilling over impregnable armour like water off a duck's back. In one last desperate bid to reach him, she cried, "I've made myself vulnerable to you by opening up like this. Can't you meet me halfway?"

It hit some chord in him. The impassivity gave way to a look of soul-weary derision. "Why does it take a crisis in our lives to force us to reevaluate where we are and what we most want?" he mused more than asked.

Joanna flushed with guilty shame. But for her pregnancy she might never have come back to Rory, never confessed her feelings for him. And he knew it.

"You ask me to meet you halfway," he continued, his eyes probing hers with merciless purpose. "Tell me, Joanna, how many times in the past three years have you evaluated? How many times since you turned your back on me and our marriage did you try to meet me halfway?"

She could not hold his gaze. In wretched defeat she turned her head aside and stared out to the relentless roll of the sea. "I didn't," she acknowledged huskily.

"Precisely. And when this crisis passes, what then, Joanna? Will you remember why you came back to me, or will the old pattern of thinking cloud your feelings again?"

She faced him in a despairing effort to offer appeasement. "Rory, I promise—"

"You broke the last promises you made to me."

"You broke them first," she defended.

"No. I didn't," he stated bitingly. "You chose not to listen to me. You still choose not to listen to me."

Joanna could feel the blood draining from her face as she recollected that he had told her yesterday that he had never been unfaithful to her. She had no defence. None at all.

"Now, how would you like your eggs done?" he drawled.

"Poached," she choked out.

He brought her breakfast. They ate the meal together. They did not touch each other's minds or hearts or hands. After a long tense silence, Rory said very quietly, "This won't do, Joanna."

"What do you mean by that?" she asked, despair sharpening her voice. He hadn't given it a chance yet. He couldn't have changed his mind already, could he? Her eyes searched his in fearful uncertainty, and her stomach fluttered in panic at the decisive purpose she read in them.

"I mean we're not at ease. We're not comfortable together," he stated flatly.

"What do you intend to do about it?" Joanna knew she had no weapons to fight whatever was on his mind, and it was obvious he had a plan of some kind.

"How do you feel today?" he asked obliquely.

"Fine."

"Are you up to visiting? It will probably take a long time."

"Yes." A sense of fatalism gripped her. Whatever his purpose was, she would rather meet it head-on and get it over and done with.

"There's a woman I want you to meet."

Joanna's heart sank. Another woman.

A bitter sense of fairness forced the reminder that she had had Brad. But she wasn't carrying Brad's child. And whoever the woman was in Rory's life, *she* wasn't carrying Rory's child.

A deep and primitive determination stirred. She was not going to give Rory up. Not to some lover he had in the wings, or any other woman. He belonged to her. He belonged to their baby. And that was how it was going to end if she had to fight for the rest of her life for it.

With a fierce possessiveness in her heart, Joanna faced Rory squarely and said, "I'm ready to meet your woman any time you like!"

CHAPTER TWELVE

JOANNA DRESSED to kill. No way was she going to give Rory's other woman the slightest advantage over her if she could help it. She put on her most expensive outfit, a stylish black suit that featured yellow buttons and yellow panels in the figure-fitting jacket. Her make-up was sophisticated without being flashy, and she brushed her blonde hair into a gleaming bounce around her shoulders.

Uncertainty twisted her stomach when she found Rory a picture of sartorial splendour in a smart charcoal suit. He had never bothered dressing like that for her. She grimly reasoned that he had not had the money to clothe himself in that fashion until recent times. The problem was, he looked so devastatingly handsome it was more than uncertainty twisting up her insides.

She wanted him. She wanted him so badly she felt sick with it. And he was not unmoved by her appearance, either, she noted with satisfaction. There was a definite glitter in his eyes when they finished skating over her.

"Ready?" he asked.

"Any time," she replied boldly.

A hot glitter, quickly hooded, but she had seen enough to know he still found her desirable whatever else he felt about her. It gave Joanna a warm glow until they were settled in his Jaguar and on their way.

"How far is it?" she asked.

"Parramatta."

Joanna frowned. Parramatta was the business centre of the western suburbs, on the opposite side of the city to Dee Why. It was hardly a handy place for Rory to have a woman. She wondered how often they met. Did they work together? If they did, she would put a stop to it. After all, if Rory didn't want her to work with Brad, he couldn't expect her to accept an ex-lover working with him.

Despite her bravado, Joanna was a mangle of nerves when Rory finally parked the car in a quiet street that was part of a new subdivision. It was lined with modest homes that wouldn't cost the earth for young married couples. She didn't know what she had expected, but it wasn't this kind of neighbourhood. Was the woman a widow? Divorced like Rory? Did she have children who were fond of him?

Joanna recoiled from that last thought, fiercely telling herself not to cross bridges until she came to them. She watched Rory round the car to her side. He looked preoccupied, but not tense or nervous. When he opened her door, it took all of Joanna's willpower to step out with some semblance of confident composure.

"What's going to happen?" she asked, needing some clue to Rory's intentions.

He shrugged. "I have no idea."

The closed look on his face did not invite further inquiry. Joanna had the impression he was leaving it entirely up to her as to what would happen. If this was to be some kind of challenge about where he stood with her, Joanna vowed to pass with flying colours.

Rory escorted her to the front porch of a small brick veneer house. He pressed the doorbell and stood back, slightly behind Joanna as though to stop her from any inclination to bolt at the last minute.

Pride stiffened her resolve. Before this day was over, she would smash every barrier between her and Rory. He would see that she meant their marriage to work as it should.

The door in front of her opened.

Joanna's mind reeled with shock. She stared in horror at the woman who stood there, the woman who had caused her so much pain, the woman who had declared Rory the father of her baby, the woman who had broken up their marriage with her pregnancy.

Bernice Lawler's pretty face reflected the same shock and horror that Joanna felt. "Oh, my God!" she gasped, her hand flying up to her mouth as though to smother her appalled reaction.

"Hello, Bernice," Rory said with a calm blandness that drove fear into the woman's eyes.

"What are you doing here?" she cried. "How did you know..."

"Where you were?" Rory finished for her. "I always kept track of you, Bernice. I was not about to lose the one person who could right the wrong that was done to me."

"But I'm married now." She looked from Rory to Joanna and back to him with anguished eyes. "You can't—"

"Mess up your life as you messed up ours?" Rory fired at her. "Believe me. I'll do my damnedest to achieve precisely that if I don't get what I want from you today."

"What's that?" she asked, panicked by the threat hanging over her.

"Tell Joanna the truth," Rory demanded.

"My husband will be home soon," she pleaded. "He only went out for a short time."

"Then there's not a moment to be wasted if you don't want him to know what you did, Bernice," Rory pressed.

"You'd better come in," she decided hastily, standing back to let them through the doorway.

Joanna was still suffering from shock. It took a slight nudge in the back from Rory to get her moving forward. Her body stiffened as she stepped past Bernice Lawler, whose voluptuous curves were clearly outlined by stretch jeans and a figure-hugging sweater. It was difficult to keep reminding herself that Rory had not been intimate with Bernice. Joanna had believed it for so long, she could not dispel the sense of threat she felt.

She found herself in a small living room furnished with the barest home comforts, a sofa, one large armchair, two beanbags, a coffee table and a television set. Shaken by being faced with the worst spectre from the past, Joanna sank onto the sofa without waiting for an invitation to sit down. Rory remained standing, retaining his iron grasp on the situation.

Having closed the door behind them, Bernice skirted her nemesis and moved over to the armchair. She was far too agitated to sit. She flicked her long brown hair behind her shoulders, pushed at her fringe, folded her arms in a defensive hug that made her full breasts jut over them. Her thickly lashed amber eyes darted from Rory to Joanna, hating their intrusion on her life and home, but forced to accept it.

"Look! It was a bad time in my life," she started resentfully.

"It was a bad time in our lives, too," Joanna bit out, churning with a surge of anger she could barely control.

"You think so?" Bernice scoffed. "You had it made with a man who had eyes only for you. No matter how much I tried to make myself more attractive to him, he never took any notice of me. He only saw me as one of his employees."

"And for that you lied about your pregnancy?" Joanna shot at her, incredulous that an unencouraged infatuation could drive a woman to such lengths.

"No." Bernice's chin jerked up at a defiant angle. "I *was* pregnant "

"Was Rory the father?" Joanna demanded.

There was a long pause before Bernice answered. Her eyes drifted away, taking on an unseeing quality. "No," she said finally, heavily. "Mr. Grayson was not the father of that child. He never touched me."

Was she lying? There was something wrong here. Joanna flicked a glance at Rory. He was looking at

Bernice, his brow furrowed. He was not accepting the pat answer with any equanimity. It didn't satisfy him, either. It left too much unanswered.

Joanna couldn't sit still. She stood up, her whole body taut with the need to know. "Then why, Bernice?" she asked curtly. "Why did you put us through the hell you did?"

"It's your own fault," Bernice flashed at her, a sharp hostility brightening her eyes as they targeted Joanna. "You should have believed your husband." Again her chin jerked up defiantly. "If I had my life over again, I'd probably do the same."

Joanna struggled to stay calm in the face of such unbalanced reasoning. She forced her voice to a quiet, even tenor as she stated her position. "I admit I should have believed my husband. At the time I believed your story. I didn't think a woman would make such a serious accusation unless it was true."

"Then you've lived a very sheltered life, Mrs. Grayson," Bernice mocked. "A lucky life."

"Did *I* do something that hurt you?" Joanna asked, trying her utmost to come to grips with the situation.

Her only reply was a wild, derisive laugh.

"Why did you want to cause such trouble between us, Bernice?" Joanna persisted. "Did you think Rory might turn to you if I was out of the picture?"

The bitter laughter died into a blaze of dark, turbulent hatred. "Have you ever been raped, Mrs. Grayson?"

"No," Joanna answered, taken aback by the violence of feeling emanating from Bernice Lawler.

"Well, I was. I went to a party and met a man with the kind of easy charm your husband has. Tall, dark and handsome. I thought I was lucky for once. Really lucky. Like you, Mrs. Grayson. But I was only a *thing* to him. A *thing* he could use like the animal he was. I begged and cried and pleaded but he didn't care. He only cared about getting what *he* wanted out of me. Do you know what that feels like?"

"No," Joanna murmured.

"Well, I know how I felt. Dirty. Degraded. Reduced to nothing. Men were animals. And I was their victim. When I found out he'd made me pregnant on top of everything else he'd done to me, I selected a victim for myself."

Her eyes turned their savage glitter onto Rory. "He was just like him. Handsome and charming on the surface but not giving a damn about me as a person. I hated him for not seeing my real worth. I was just a *thing* who worked for him. I saw no reason he shouldn't pay for the child that one of his kind had forced upon me."

Rory shook his head. "Then I failed you, too, Bernice, that you should feel that of me," he said quietly.

"You don't care about me. You never did. And you don't now. You only care about her." Her gaze swung to Joanna in fierce belligerence. "And you believed me. You believed he was capable of doing what I said he did. So I was justified in picking on him."

"No," Joanna said softly. "But I do understand why you didn't care what harm you did. And I'm sorry that you suffered so much."

The rage suddenly crumpled into tears. "Please don't hurt me now. I love my husband. He's a good man. And you two are back together again."

"Yes, we are," Joanna agreed, feeling intensely grateful that Rory was prepared to give her another chance.

She felt drained of all the bitter hostility that Bernice Lawler had evoked in her. She was painfully conscious that she shared the blame for what had happened. If she had stood by Rory and believed in his love for her, the other woman could never have succeeded in destroying their marriage. She stepped over and gave Bernice's arm a reassuring squeeze.

"We'll go now. We'll never come back. I hope you'll be very happy with your husband."

Bernice turned a frightened face to Rory. "My husband doesn't know. We're having a baby. One I can love this time. And we've been so happy."

"I have no wish to harm you, Bernice," he said gravely. "I'm sorry that another man did."

Moved by their unexpected sympathy, she broke into a fresh bout of weeping, shaking her head in distress as words of shame tumbled from her lips. "I'm sorry, too. About you and your wife. I'm glad you came. It's been on my conscience so long. I felt so guilty. But I tried not to think of it. Tried to pretend it never happened. I couldn't—" her eyes begged their forgiveness "—I just couldn't make myself face up to it."

"It's over now," Rory assured her.

"Could you please go before my husband comes back?" she begged.

They left in a silence that needed relief from the catharsis of revelations that had been festering in secrecy far too long. Rory drove until they came to an old established public park with massive trees and gardens aglow with rows of primulas and cinerarias.

He stopped the car and alighted without any word to Joanna. Nor did he speak when he helped her out of the passenger seat. He took her hand, his fingers closing tightly around hers, drawing her with him to stroll slowly together over an expanse of green lawn to one of the park benches.

It was precisely what they needed, Joanna thought, the sense of peaceful beauty, of nature being allowed to grow and bloom, untainted by any pollution or vandalism. It washed away the taste of ugliness, of the perversion of evil, and renewed the hope for how things should be. It brought home to Joanna the deep inner sensitivity that she had loved in Rory, and for the first time since their re-meeting, she felt her soul attuned to his, as it had once been in the flower of their youth.

How they had lost it she could not remember, but it had dissipated somewhere along the track of their marriage well before Bernice Lawler had come on the scene. If it had remained strong, nothing could have broken the bond between them. Somehow they had let it fray, and Joanna could now acknowledge that much of it was her fault.

They sat on the hard wooden slats of the bench, welcoming the feeling of lasting solidity beneath them. Synthetic comfort had no place here. Joanna looked up at the intertwining branches of trees that had accommodated each other's growth, allowing coexistence without mutual destruction.

"I've been so wrong," she said sadly, regretfully.

"Haven't we all?" Rory murmured. "In one way or another."

She looked at him, seeing Rory Grayson for all that he was to her, generous of heart, open of mind, the sexiest man she had ever known. And she cursed herself for the blindness she had cultivated through her lack of faith in his love, the blindness that had cast him into the worst possible light because she couldn't accept her own failings.

"Forgive me?" she whispered.

The pained understanding in his eyes humbled her further. "There's nothing to forgive, Joanna," he said with a rueful little smile. "In your place I would probably have done the same. The one saving grace of our marriage, however bad it got, was knowing that above and beyond everything that went wrong, you were mine. Take that away..." He shook his head.

"I'm sorry about Brad, Rory. He was..."

"I had other women, Joanna. After the divorce."

"I know."

His expression turned quizzical. "You kept tabs on me?"

"No. But the bathrobe you lent me had been worn before."

He grimaced, his eyes reflecting a sad understanding of how such a telling detail might have affected her. "We all make mistakes, Joanna," he said on a soft note of appeal.

She nodded. Given her own mistakes, it was easy to dismiss his. But there was one question that had plagued her mind from the first moment he had shown her into his apartment. "Why did you create our dream home, Rory?"

A whimsical little smile played over his mouth. "I guess I couldn't quite kill the hope that one day you would come back to me."

But not pregnant, Joanna thought, not driven back to him because of a child they had created together. Did he accept that her love for him had never really died? That she wanted him as her husband and partner in life, and that being the father of her children was only part of the whole picture?

"Is everything going to be right for the future now?" she asked, careful not to presume too much. Then on a note of yearning she could not suppress, "Can we turn the clock back to where we once were, Rory?"

Determination flashed into his eyes. "I don't want to go back and live through the same mistakes again, Joanna. I want to move forward on much sounder ground."

"Do you think we can do that?" she asked, hope soaring in her heart.

"Yes. I'm certain of it."

Relief flooded through her, lighting her face with a glow of happiness.

"But there is one more visit we have to make today," Rory said with grim purpose.

Joanna's glow was instantly dimmed. "I don't think I can deal with many more shocks like Bernice," she appealed.

"I doubt that you'll get one."

"Whom do you want me to see?" Joanna asked warily.

He paused, took a deep breath, then on a long weary sigh came the words, "Your mother."

CHAPTER THIRTEEN

APPARENTLY Rory was determined on laying all the ghosts of their past marriage to rest today, one way or another. Despite her break from her mother, it seemed that he still perceived Fay Harding as some kind of threat to their happiness together. If he needed reassurance, then...

"Do you want to set off now?" she asked.

"If you're ready," he replied, his eyes watchful for any uncertainty in hers.

Joanna rose from the park bench and gave him a perky smile. "Well, Mum can hardly look down upon you now as an impecunious ne'er-do-well."

His responding smile had a sardonic curl as he stood and made a mocking point of straightening his silk tie. "You think I'll pass muster?"

Joanna felt her cheeks start to flame as she realised he *had* dressed for her. In their courting days she had appealed to him to make some effort to dress in a way that didn't offend her mother's standards.

His stock reply, "Clothes do not make the man, Joanna", made no concession for the sake of peace. It was a fair statement. Joanna conceded it, believed it, but it didn't help with her mother. Not that anything would have, Joanna now realised. Her mother had been dead set against Rory from the start.

She raised pained eyes to the gentle mockery in his. "What my mother thinks about you doesn't matter, Rory. Not to me. We'll live our lives as we see fit."

He lifted a hand and tenderly stroked her hot cheek. "It's all right, Joanna. I'm older, and I hope wiser now. I don't need to prove anything about myself anymore, so I don't mind giving in to others' needs. Within reason."

"If she doesn't accept you—"

Rory slid his fingers to her lips. "Let's wait and see."

Half an hour later they were outside Jessica's house in Burwood. Every Sunday Fay Harding went to her younger daughter's home for lunch. Rory had not needed to be directed here. He remembered. In years gone by, Jessica had braved their mother's disapproval several times to invite Joanna and Rory to her and Philip's home. It had been such a strained social situation, Joanna had begged off Jessica's attempts at family get-togethers rather than cause trouble between her sister and her mother.

The solid brick home was of standard Federation design, brick pillars supporting the conventional veranda. It was set off by a neat conventional garden that somehow reflected the old adage, a place for everything and everything in its place.

Joanna was suddenly assailed by a sick, helpless feeling as she and Rory approached the front door. If her mother forced her to a decision where she had to choose, she had no doubt in her mind what that decision was going to be. Her future lay with Rory, and her first loyalty was to him. Yet her mother was still her mother. It hurt to be rejected. It hurt to have to reject. If only her mother could see, could accept that Rory was the right man for her... but that was wishing for the moon.

Philip, Jessica's husband, answered the doorbell. "Joanna," he greeted her in surprise, then more in shock, "Rory!"

"May we come in, Philip?" Joanna asked, struggling to attain a detached frame of mind, determined to remain calm and dignified, no matter what provocation was offered.

It flustered him. Philip Denning was a neat, conventional man faced with highly unexpected visitors who would undoubtedly create chaos out of his neat, conventional Sunday.

Rory thrust out his hand, and Philip's ingrained good manners made him automatically meet it with his. "Good to see you again, Philip," Rory said forcefully, and the decision to welcome them or not slid into the too-hard basket.

Rory swept Joanna past Philip, and since their being inside was a fait accompli, Philip closed the door behind them and weakly waved them into the living room.

This was an L-shaped area, comprising both dining room and sitting room. The table was set with five places for lunch, which was always served promptly at twelve-thirty. It was almost that now, and the voices of Joanna's sister, mother and two little nieces were clearly audible from the direction of the kitchen.

"Who was that, Philip?" Jessica called out.

He cleared his throat. "It's Joanna, dear," he replied, clearly funking the announcement of Rory's arrival with her.

The childish babble continued. The adult voices cut out. Philip had not recollected himself enough to invite Joanna and Rory to sit down, so all three of them were still standing when the rest of the family came into the room to greet Joanna. Jessica stopped dead in her tracks when she saw Rory. Her daughters were too young to have any memory of him, so they eyed him with childish curiosity as they ran forward to Joanna. She was bending down to give them a hug and a kiss when her mother made her appearance.

"Jessica, Mrs. Harding," Rory rolled out smoothly, taking their shock at seeing him in his stride.

"It's ... it's good to see you, Rory. Joanna," Jessica said, looking to her sister uncertainly, clearly wondering what this visit meant.

Joanna's mother did not return any greeting. The little girls fell silent, sensing something wrong. They trailed to Jessica and hung onto her skirt for security. Joanna straightened up, watching her mother's reaction and fiercely willing her not to be hostile.

Fay Harding stared at Rory, her face completely blank of all expression. Then slowly her gaze turned to Joanna, an uncertain, searching look that seemed to plead for some reversal of the situation. Joanna moved closer to Rory, making her position clear. He put his arm around her waist, making their togetherness clear to everyone.

Philip jerked into action. "Shall I get us all a drink?"

"No, thank you, Philip," Rory said quietly. "Joanna and I didn't come to impose on your hospitality. We only wish to make an announcement."

"Oh! Right!" Philip muttered, still hopelessly at sea about what to do.

"Mrs. Harding, you know that Joanna came to me some weeks ago," Rory said with a directness that commanded attention. "She asked if bygones could be bygones. Today I would like to ask that of you. Of all of you. And the reason I ask is because Joanna and I are getting married again, and you are her family."

He paused to give them time to absorb what this meant to them and decide on how to act. No-one said anything. There was no rush of congratulations. Philip looked intensely uncomfortable, not knowing where to cast his eyes. Jessica looked incredulously at Joanna, not having had any warning of a reconciliation. Her mother stared fixedly at Rory, showing no emotion whatsoever.

"Furthermore," Rory went on, "we have other good news for you. Joanna is going to have a baby. My baby."

Another deathly silence, strangling any hope that something might change to accommodate Joanna and Rory in the family circle. Rory waited. Joanna waited. Each passing second thickened the bleak resignation that was settling in Joanna's soul. Not even her baby merited a token welcome.

"Well," said Philip, then harumphed, completely nonplussed about how to be a model of tact.

"I'm glad," Jessica suddenly leapt in with surprising strength. Her voice wavered slightly as she added, "If it's what you want, Joanna."

"Yes, it is," Joanna affirmed, shooting a grateful look at her younger sister.

Jessica then took the bull by the horns and appealed to their mother. "Mum, please... Joanna's been so good to you. Be fair to her."

Fay Harding gave no response. It was as though she had looked upon the hissing snakes of Medusa's head and been turned to stone.

"Last, but not least," Rory drawled with unruffled aplomb. "While all the details will be left up to Joanna, of course, as is her right, I can give you an overall picture of what is to happen."

Hugging Joanna firmly to his side, he turned her with him and guided her to directly face Philip, who was forced into looking straight at both of them.

"I'm sorry if we've embarrassed you, Philip," Rory said with appealing sincerity. "That was neither my intention nor Joanna's. Like me, you're simply an add-on to this family. And none of what has happened is your fault."

He started to move Joanna forward, paused, then wagged a finger at the hideous vase that dominated one side of the mantelpiece. It was in the shape of a huge fish sitting on its tail and with its thick-lipped mouth gulping open. "Always hated that damned thing! I bet you do, too, Philip. Why don't you smash it to smithereens? It's unworthy of your taste."

With a smooth turn of direction, Rory brought Joanna face to face with her sister.

"Thank you for your kind acceptance, Jessica," he said warmly. "I don't want Joanna cut off from her family as she was before, but we don't want to make trouble between you and your mother, either. We'll understand if you choose...whatever way you choose."

Jessica looked hard at him. "My sister needs some real happiness, Rory. I just hope you're going to give her what she needs."

"It won't be for want of trying on my part," he assured her.

Rory didn't allow Joanna time to say anything to her sister. He swept her on to take the last stand with him, in front of her mother.

"You know, Mrs. Harding," he started pleasantly, "when Joanna and I were first married, it was in a registry office. We couldn't afford the splendour of what Jessica and Philip were able to enjoy. But I'm perfectly willing to let bygones be bygones, and to forget what happened. This time we're going to have a wedding that will give Joanna every dream she ever had about her wedding day."

There was a slight jerk of Fay Harding's head, as though she did not want to hear what Rory was saying, but he drove on with quietly measured force, relentlessly holding her a captive audience to his speech.

"If Joanna wants a church wedding it will be in the church of her choice. If she wants to be married in a garden, it will be the finest garden in this country. If she wants to be married on a luxury liner, we'll have it on the QE2. Whatever she wants, and more, I will give it to her. And you're all invited to the wedding if you wish to come."

He glanced around at the others, then back to her mother, who remained rigidly silent, her face pale and pinched.

"We'll come," Jessica said emphatically. "We'll all come, won't we, Mum? Joanna came to you when you wanted her."

The strong appeal fell on deaf ears.

"You see, Mrs. Harding," Rory continued, "whatever you may think of me, I love your daughter. And there is one thing I can promise. It will be, at least for us, and especially for Joanna—" he paused, then said with a low throb of passionate avowal "—a wedding to remember."

It drew Joanna's gaze to his, and she found his eyes burning with the determination to erase bad memories and replace them with good. It moved her deeply that he should care so much about making this right for her. "I love you too, Rory," she declared softly, wanting him to know, wanting to say it in front of her mother.

He smiled, a warm, beautiful satisfaction glowing at her, then he slowly turned his smile to her mother. "That's all I have to say, Mrs. Harding."

He gave a slight bow of his head and started to turn away. Joanna stopped him, appealing for his patience. "There's something I wish to say."

"Whatever you want."

She looked at her mother, who had been so closely entwined with most of her life. She made one last desperate search for the love she had yearned for, the giving kind of love that didn't have any price on it. She found nothing but a blank emptiness looking back at her.

"I'm sorry I failed you, Mum," she said sadly. "I'm sorry I wasn't the daughter you wanted. I'm sorry that the values you hold so dear are not my values. But in the end, I have to be me."

Then suddenly the blankness cracked, and instead of emptiness there was the tortured recognition of finality in her mother's eyes. She knew this was her last chance of reaching across the gulf that now separated them. Her lips trembled, but she rose to the occasion, splendidly, magnificently, as only a mother can, drawing from her soul the gift of truth, sacrificing her pride, speaking from a heart torn by things she didn't want to say, but forcing herself to say them.

"I loved you too much, Joanna," she began in a tremulous burst. "And I used that love to strangle you, to hold you back, to keep you as mine. I realise that now. Since you walked out that night, I came to understand what I had done. And all in the name of love. You have nothing to be sorry about. Nor to regret. You've given me far more than I deserved from you."

Anguish twisted across her face. "And Rory, too. All I could do was pick at him for taking my daughter away from me. I was jealous of your love for him, of the joy he gave you. I didn't want to see any good in him. I'm sorry. Terribly sorry. . ."

She choked into silence as tears welled to her eyes. Joanna threw her arms around her mother and hugged her tight.

"It's okay, Mum," she soothed. "I know how love can get all twisted around."

As hers had done with Rory. Her eyes pleaded for his understanding and forgiveness, and true to his generous nature, he put his arms around both of them, giving the ground for a bridge to be built.

The peacemaking would have been awkward but for Rory's amazing ability to turn any situation around. In no time at all he had Philip pouring drinks for everyone, promoting a spirit of bonhomie. Jessica was only too happy to fall in with Rory's appeal to stretch the roast leg of lamb to seven servings, and he warmly praised her superb cooking. Joanna won a glow of warm delight from her sister by saying she would love to have her two little nieces as flower girls at the wedding.

Everyone was gently solicitous of Fay Harding's comfort and needs. She remained quiet for the most part. When she did venture a comment or a question, it was either a genuine attempt to mend her attitude towards Rory, or a tentative appeal to Joanna to be involved with the wedding plans, at least in a helping capacity. Both Rory and Joanna met her more than halfway.

It was mid-afternoon when they took their leave of the family. For the first time in many years, Joanna felt a strong surge of unreserved love and respect for her mother as she kissed her goodbye. She hugged Jessica, as well, moved by a new warmth between them.

The sound of crashing china in the living room drew their startled attention. They all looked to see a benign smile spreading across Philip's face as he strolled over to join them.

"Funny thing to happen," he said innocently. "The fish vase just fell off the mantel."

"But that was a wedding present from Aunt Phoebe!" Jessica cried.

"Well, I'm afraid it's unfixable, dear."

Jessica started to smile, then sputtered into a mad giggle. "I never liked it, either."

Then they were all laughing, and it was on a wave of gloriously light-hearted humour that Joanna and Rory finally drove away.

Joanna sighed her contentment. She turned to the man at her side with implicit trust in his judgement. "Will it last, Rory?"

He threw her a warming smile. "I think so. But if it doesn't, we gave your family their chance to be part of our family."

"Yes." She reached over and lovingly stroked his thigh. "Thank you for everything."

He cocked a wicked eyebrow at her. "Keep doing that and I'll drive straight into the bedroom."

"What a splendid idea!" Her eyes danced her delight in him. "I adore you, Rory Grayson."

"Likewise, Joanna Harding."

"Does this mean I don't have to sleep alone on my side of the bed tonight?" she asked archly.

"No. It means that I don't have to sleep alone on *my* side of the bed. Ever again!"

They ended up using both sides of the bed in a long celebration of their love for each other, a love that was far richer and more precious for having been lost and found again.

CHAPTER FOURTEEN

JOANNA DECIDED on a castle for their wedding. The one she fancied had been built by an eccentric millionaire at the turn of the century. It stood in a commanding position, overlooking Sydney Harbour from the long-established northern suburb of Hunters Hill. It was now in use as a function centre that specialised in weddings.

Castles, Joanna found, did not come cheaply. This one was outrageously expensive, but Rory didn't turn a hair at the proposed cost. He called the inquiries number straight away and booked the entire complex for the first suitable date available.

Joanna's mother helped her with the invitations, and they pored over bride magazines together, looking at hundreds of designs for bridal parties. Since Isaac Stone was going to be Rory's best man, Joanna asked Monique to be chief matron of honour. She was fast becoming friends with the lively brunette who endeared herself to Joanna with many neighbourly kindnesses.

Jessica and Philip were delighted when they also were asked to join the formal bridal party as second matron of honour and groomsman. Having their two little daughters as flower girls made it very much a family affair.

In the weeks leading up to the wedding, the only glitch in Joanna's happiness was the letter she received from Poppy Dalton. She had written Poppy a long, excited account of all that had happened with Rory, as well as inviting her to the big day at the castle, and the reply that came back absolutely floored Joanna in its unexpectedness.

Dear Joanna,

I am so pleased that you're back with Rory and you're getting married again. He is a very special person. The news about the baby is wonderful. I would love to go to your wedding, and I will certainly be thinking of you on the day and wishing you every happiness.

However, I must, with deep regret, decline your invitation, Joanna.

You see, miracle of miracles, Brad Latham has taken an interest in me and we've been keeping company almost since the new school term began. I'm quite mad about him. Always have been, if the truth be told. And we're already talking about getting married in the Christmas vacation. I know it sounds too fast, especially after his long relationship with you. Brad says he's surprised at himself. But we're amazingly happy together, so I hope you can wish us happiness.

It was only with your help, and Rory's, that this change in my life became possible, so I am deeply grateful to you both for guiding me into giving myself the best chance at the future I wanted.

Love,
Poppy

Joanna spent the rest of the day shaking her head and feeling quite disturbed about Poppy's future. As soon as Rory came home from work, she handed him the letter without comment.

He quickly perused it, then raised one eyebrow inquiringly. "Does it worry you?"

"Only in so far as it concerns Poppy. Will she be happy?"

"I think so."

"What makes you so sure, Rory? I think Brad wants a wife to help in his career. What if he's taken up with Poppy simply because she's there and available?"

Rory considered the question for a moment, then slowly shook his head. "I doubt that it matters in the long run, Joanna."

"How can you say that?" she protested.

He took her hand and drew her with him. "Come and look at the stars with me," he murmured.

It was a crisp, clear evening. As they strolled along the terrace, breathing in the fresh sea air and pausing between the arches to admire the brightness of the early twilight stars, Rory said, "You remember the night when I adopted the alias of Isaac Stone?"

"I'll never forget it," Joanna assured him ruefully.

"Poppy and I had a long talk. We spoke of secret dreams and hopes." He paused, smiling whimsically.

"Maybe that's my forte in life. To cast light on dark places."

Her eyes caressed him with warm appreciation. "You certainly do that, Rory."

He leaned against the railing and looked down at the shifting swell of the sea. "Poppy had a yearning for Brad. He was her dream. I gave her a number of options for how to go about attracting his attention and interest."

"So that's what she meant about you helping her."

"People are people the world over," Rory mused quietly. "They like to be listened to. They like to feel someone cares about them and their problems. It could be that Poppy has struck a very real chord of need in Brad. And if she fulfils his needs, he may well grow to love her as much as she loves him."

"What about her needs?"

"They're wrapped up in Brad, Joanna. A partner in life, sharing the same kind of interests. A husband to give her children and support." He turned to her with a confident smile. "I'd say Brad will adore Poppy by the time they've had their second child. I don't think he could fail to appreciate all she'll give him, her staunch support, her kindness and compassion and understanding, her absolute loyalty."

"I hope so, Rory," Joanna said fervently.

He slid his arms around her and pulled her into a tender embrace. "There are no certainties in life, my darling. Only chances. It's up to Poppy and Brad to fulfil their dreams, just as it's up to us and everyone else to fulfil the potential of the dreams we all have, whatever they are."

ONE OF JOANNA'S DREAMS could not have been more
beautifully and magically fulfilled than her wedding
day. Winter had given way to spring, and clear bright
sunshine added its sparkle to the magnificent trees and
gardens in the grounds that surrounded the castle. The
majestic steps that curved up to the entrance were lined
with huge urns in which were planted standard ice-
berg roses in full bloom.

Inside the castle chapel, Purcell's "Trumpet Vol-
untary," followed by a fanfare, announced the arrival of the bride. In the foyer Joanna's mother checked
everyone over to make sure nothing was wrong or out
of place. Then with one last proud and loving smile at
her firstborn daughter, she turned and walked into the
chapel to take her place in the front stall.

The organ started playing Mendelssohn's "Wedding March." Jessica orchestrated the setting off down
the aisle for each of her small daughters. They had
garlands of spring flowers in their hair, baskets of
them in their hands. Their puff-sleeved apricot satin
dresses with extravagant ruffles around the neckline
and hemline had a double skirt at the back where the
satin curved up to the waist to reveal rows and rows of
apricot lace.

The romantic old-world charm of the flower girls'
dresses was followed by more sophisticated elegance
for the matrons of honour, but the romantic flavour
was repeated in their deeper apricot sheath dresses.
Extended bodices of beaded lace flowers and diago-
nal sashes of ruched satin drew the eye to the high
ruffled sleeves that framed sweetheart necklines. Both

Monique and Jessica looked stunning as they made their measured entrance.

Joanna did not have a father to accompany her down the aisle. He had died while she was still in high school. She hadn't wanted an uncle to take his place. She preferred to give herself away to the man she loved. When the moment came for her to step forward, she did so alone, but her step was sure and steady, and she knew she wasn't alone. Rory was waiting for her. And her whole family was here to see her married to him.

Her wedding gown was one of classic simplicity, a white satin sheath with a wide shawl collar and long fitted sleeves. A train fell from the back of her waist to flow out on the aisle behind her. Her veil billowed out and flowed far beyond the train. She carried a ribboned trail of white camellias, their shiny, dark green leaves softened by little sprays of baby's breath. On her earlobes and around her neck she wore the beautiful pearls that Rory had given her as a wedding present.

A hush fell over the packed chapel as Joanna slowly made her way up the aisle to Rory, who looked wonderfully dashing in white bow tie and tails. Everywhere she glanced there were smiling faces. Far off to one side was the cameraman Rory had hired to video the ceremony. There would be nothing forgotten about this day.

Then she was beside Rory, taking his hand, and his eyes were telling her she was the bride of his heart and soul and body, always was, always would be, but especially so here and now. The marriage celebrant began the service. Joanna had chosen a traditional ceremony. She liked the old words. To her they had poetry and meaning. There were readings from the Bible, a choir singing hymns that lifted the heart and made it soar, and finally the solemn vows repeated by her and Rory to make them husband and wife again.

The signing of the register was followed by the playing of the triumphant grand march from *Aïda* as the bridal party slowly made their way out of the chapel to the acclaim of all who had gathered to witness the wedding.

Formal photographs were taken in the castle grounds while guests milled happily around, being served champagne and hors d'oeuvres by an army of waiters. The video man worked overtime to capture everyone and everything on film.

They were posed under an arch of wisteria, arranged more casually beside an ornamental pond where a school of goldfish had the flower girls fascinated, posed again beneath a huge plane tree, and finally on the steps to the castle. By this time the guests had been ushered inside. Once the last formal photographs were taken, Philip and Jessica hurried their daughters off to a rest room. Monique and Isaac lingered with Joanna and Rory, who declared he had a pose in mind that he wanted to have captured for posterity.

His vivid blue eyes twinkled wickedly at Joanna. "I think it only fitting that I add my personal stamp on this wedding to remember."

Whereupon he gathered her close to him, then bent her extravagantly over his arm in the most cavalier

ravishing style, and began kissing her throat, mur-
muring words of passionate intent. Joanna could not
help laughing. She threw her head back and felt a
breeze lift her long veil into a floating cloud of freedom that somehow enhanced the mad, glorious moment with Rory.

She was vaguely aware of the cameraman clicking
as fast as his finger would go and Isaac and Monique
laughing in the background, but it was a high, urgent
voice calling out that broke the mood.

"Mr. Stone! Mr. Stone!"

The tone gave warning that something was wrong.
Rory instantly swept Joanna upright with him and
they turned to look at the man, who was now paused
at the foot of the steps, puffing from the exertion of
hurrying, his face as red as a beetroot. He was a ro-
tund little man, almost bald, middle-aged, and dressed
in a very dapper fashion, a fob watch and chain
looped across the waistcoat of a navy pinstripe suit,
and a high-collared shirt cutting into a roll of fat
around his neck.

As he used a handkerchief to mop his glistening
brow, Joanna looked at Isaac for enlightenment. Isaac
had his eyebrows raised questioningly at Monique. She
shrugged her ignorance of the stranger's identity.
None the wiser, they all stared down at the little man,
who, having caught his breath and captured their attention, advanced up the steps directly towards Rory.

"Mr. Stone..." He glanced from Rory to Joanna
and back again. A forlorn, lost note crept into his
voice. "I couldn't find you. I looked everywhere I

could think of." He cast another anguished glance at Joanna. "And now I think I'm too late."

"Who," said Rory, looking as nonplussed as the rest of them, "are you?"

"The name's Kawowski," the little man announced self-importantly. "Joseph Kawowski."

Joanna barely smothered a groan. Not again, she thought incredulously. The man was becoming her nemesis.

On a surge of triumph, Joseph Kawowski declared, "I've found your perfect match, Mr. Stone!"

Joanna heard Rory say, "It is a grave matter indeed, Mr. Kawowski. For yes, it is true. You are too late." He gave Joanna's hand a squeeze.

"Yes," she affirmed. "He's *my* husband, and I'm not going to let anyone take him away from me."

The little man shook his head in mournful reproof. "I don't know what the world is coming to. This is the second time it's happened this week. The Dalton woman, and now you, Mr. Stone. People shouldn't get married without being properly matched."

Poppy? Married to Brad already? Maybe Brad *had* surprised himself by falling head over heels in love with her, Joanna thought with a rush of warm pleasure. It was not like him to do something so impulsive.

"May I offer you a piece of advice, Mr. Kawowski?" Rory said gravely.

"By all means, Mr. Stone."

"Go to Grayson and Grayson. Ask for Monique. Sign any contract she puts in front of you. They'll put you on the right track. This will never happen to you again."

. With an air of absolute saintliness he turned to Joanna, dipped her over his arm again, then pressed an even more fervent trail of kisses up her throat.

In a blissful haze, Joanna heard Mr. Kawowski retreating in the distance, muttering as he went, "Grayson and Grayson. They'll see me right. I'll sign with them."

Gone, thought Joanna, and was promptly proven wrong.

"Mr. Stone! Why aren't you wearing your black patch? Did you get your sight back?"

Rory interrupted his kissing long enough to say, "It was a miracle of love, Mr. Kawowski," then smoothly continued where he had left off.

"A miracle," Mr. Kawowski recited dazedly as he trailed away.

Yes, a miracle, Joanna thought gratefully.

In a weird kind of way, Mr. Kawowski had brought her and Rory together, but she didn't feel inclined to tell Rory that the little man had a hand, albeit unknowingly, in their perfect match. A wife didn't have to tell a husband *everything*. She was allowed a few *tiny* secrets.

Besides, she was quite sure Mr. Kawowski had faded from Rory's mind. His lips were fervently working their way towards her mouth, and she suspected there would be such distracting activities taking up the rest of their lives.

He kissed her with passion and love. Joanna was completely certain of that love. She knew it would remain true and steady, no matter what difficulties they had to face in the future, what obstacles had to be overcome. This was the first day of their new life together, and they would make it a good life, not only for herself and Rory, but very especially for the family they would have.

"We have to go in to our guests," she murmured when Rory allowed her breath enough to murmur.

"Do we have to?" he asked.

"Don't be wicked. I told you you would have to curb yourself for a week, and a week's not up until tonight."

"In that case, we might as well go in and greet our guests." He waggled his eyebrows with villainous intent. "But beware the bridal waltz. I have a mind to make you melt onto the dance floor."

Joanna grinned. "That will undoubtedly make it a wedding to remember," she declared with delicious satisfaction.

They turned and walked through the great entrance to the castle, and Joanna's heart was singing, singing with love and peace and contentment. As she pressed closer to Rory and felt his arm tighten around her waist, she knew with absolute certainty that he, too, had found his valley of peace, and was feeling exactly the same wonderful sensations that belonged to this day of reunion and celebration.

They had a baby boy.

POSTCARDS FROM EUROPE

HARLEQUIN PRESENTS®

Travel across Europe in 1994 with Harlequin Presents. Collect a new Postcards from Europe title each month!

Don't miss
YESTERDAY'S AFFAIR
by Sally Wentworth
Harlequin Presents #1668

Available in July wherever Harlequin Presents books are sold.

HPPPE7

Hi!

I arrived safely in England and have found Nick. My feelings for him are as strong as ever, but he seems convinced that what we once shared belongs in the past. My heart won't accept that.
Love, Olivia

HARLEQUIN®

PRESENTS Plus

Beth wants a child, but she doesn't want a husband.
Enter Alex Thiarchos. She seduces him and then
vanishes—it's a simple, yet rebellious, plan.
Except that life is *never* simple!

Samantha has worked for Guy Harwood for five years,
but it isn't until he reveals his desire to be a father
that she has the courage to make him a
daring proposition....

Fall in love with Alex and Guy—Beth and Samantha do!

Watch for

A Secret Rebellion by Anne Mather
Harlequin Presents Plus #1663

and

A Daring Proposition by Miranda Lee
Harlequin Presents Plus #1664

Harlequin Presents Plus
The best has just gotten better!

Available in July wherever Harlequin books are sold.

PPLUS14

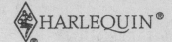

HARLEQUIN®

Harlequin Books requests the pleasure of your company this June in Eternity, Massachusetts, for WEDDINGS, INC.

For generations, couples have been coming to Eternity, Massachusetts, to exchange wedding vows. Legend has it that those married in Eternity's chapel are destined for a lifetime of happiness. And the residents are more than willing to give the legend a hand.

Beginning in June, you can experience the legend of Eternity. Watch for one title per month, across all of the Harlequin series.

HARLEQUIN BOOKS...
NOT THE SAME OLD STORY!

WEDGEN